DARE TO TR

The Dare Series 1

Dixie Lynn Dwyer

MENAGE EVERLASTING

Siren Publishing, Inc.
www.SirenPublishing.com

DEDICATION

Dear Readers,

Thank you for purchasing this legal copy of *Dare to Trust*. This new mini summer series was created with my loyal readers in mind. A fast-paced, four-book series about a new town called Chance. Located in South Carolina, this town is a bit of a secret spot where the loyalty of a close-knit community helps secure happiness as well as provide a safe haven for those on the run and looking to start a new life.

There's that special southern Carolina charm, down home cooking, and a law enforcement community ready to nip any trouble in the bud before it even starts. So hold on for the ride, as four women journey to Chance and find out that life can get worse or get better, their choice, and only if they're willing to take a chance.

Happy Reading!

Hugs!

~Dixie~

DARE TO TRUST

The Dare Series 1

DIXIE LYNN DWYER
Copyright © 2015

Chapter 1

"You have got to go out with us tonight, Marlena. We all need to let loose a little," Marlena's friend Adele said as she picked up a lunch order to bring back to the office at the construction company she worked for.

Marlena packed it up and then added the to-go cups to a carrier.

"I don't know. I'm not really in the mood. My feet hurt, I've worked doubles all week, I just want to relax."

"Well, you can definitely do that at Spencer's. We can have a few drinks, listen to the band playing, then head home early. It's just to get out a bit. I'm so tired of being kept up in that darn office all day long. I was thinking about this little trip to pick up lunch since Monday. You know how Will, Leo, and Hank don't like to order food out. They're so into their fitness and nutrition. It drives me nuts. I have to hide my bag of Doritos under my desk and sneak them into my mouth when they're not looking," Adele told her, sounding so outraged at having to do that.

Marlena chuckled. Adele seemed to be attracted to her three bosses. But who in their right mind wouldn't. They were gorgeous, wealthy, and downright mysterious. But Adele had trust issues. She admitted to that one evening at Mercedes's small house and under the influence of a great Cabernet and it was a sleepover. It was a great night but also revealed all of their weaknesses and fears. They had become best friends in such a short period of time. Marlena believed having the three women as best friends made life and dealing with her own past more bearable.

"I don't know. Let me think about it. I have four more hours to go," Marlena said then heard the chime by the front door ring and glanced to see who the next customer would be. The place was pretty damn full.

Her breath caught in her throat at the sight of Mike Spencer, the diner owner's son. He was one of three and a deputy in town. He made her nervous. Put her on edge every time he came in, and it wasn't just that damn deputy uniform either.

"I need to get moving. Enjoy lunch," she told Adele. Adele gave her a wink. Her friend knew that Mike and even his brothers made her a nervous wreck. Danny and Jack Spencer owned Spencer's dance hall and bar. That was why she tried not to go there too often.

She greeted the deputy as he held the door open for Adele and tipped his hat. As his eyes glanced over Adele and her sexy little secretary outfit—tight skirt and V-neck blouse, all in a pale blue— Marlena felt a bit crumpled. It was odd. She felt a little jealous that Mike looked at Adele like that. The sensation was quick and she didn't read into it. She lost her self-confidence and was very insecure when it came to her looks and her body. Peter had done a number on her. He'd made her feel worthless. He'd made her fearful of a man's attention, never mind touch. Hell, she feared socializing because Peter always had her on a display being critiqued by him, his associates, and any other people he asked. Alcoholism was a disease. He could have killed her.

"Good morning, Deputy Spencer. Would you like to sit at the counter or would you like a table?" she asked. He squinted those sexy blue eyes at her and she tightened her lips as she adjusted her apron, playing with the pocket in the front.

"A table would be perfect, Marlena. I'm meeting someone," he said. She nodded.

"Just let me clear that table in the corner for you. I'll be just a minute," she said and headed that way. She was shaking, the man was so attractive. She couldn't help but to wonder who he was meeting there. But as she cleared the table she felt his presence close behind her.

"Let me grab that for you," he said. Her arms were filled with dishes and a large platter still sat on the table.

"I'll come back for it. Don't sit yet. Let me wipe it down," she ordered, sounding kind of snappy. The man did that to her. He made her uptight, on edge, ready to run.

She quickly headed behind the counter to the kitchen. She placed the dirty dishes down next to the sink then looked for the rag. She added some soap and water, then grabbed a dry rag, and when she turned around, Deputy Mike Spencer was in the kitchen placing the platter down on the table by the dishwasher.

"Hey, Mike, how are you, son?" Roy Spencer asked and Mike looked at his dad then at her. He gave her a wink.

"Just grabbing breakfast."

"Danny and Jack coming?"

"I think so. I only have about thirty minutes," Mike said and glanced at Marlena. He licked his lower lip.

"I'll have the table cleaned down in a jiffy." She hurried from the kitchen.

She was shaking, she felt so nervous. Danny and Jack were joining him. All three of them in one place? All of them here?

She looked for Alice, the other waitress, but she was swamped, too. She couldn't ask her to cover this table.

Marlena cleared another table after cleaning Mike's table and placing down three place settings.

She could do this. She could handle serving the three men lunch.

She passed him on her way to the kitchen. "Can I start you off with a drink while you're waiting for the others?" she asked.

"Sure thing, doll, an ice tea with lemon."

She nodded her head and headed back to the kitchen.

* * * *

Mike Spencer felt his heart racing. Every time he saw Marlena, she did that to him. Since day one when she showed up in town, looking so sad and in need of a job. His mother noticed immediately and took a liking to Marlena. His dads, Roy and Regan, hired her on the spot. It was perfect timing, since they'd just lost one of their full-time waitresses, Cara, who was having her third baby.

Chance was a nice-size community with great people. They had everything they could ask for in a town. There wasn't a need to go out of town for much except to change up the pace of things and explore other towns and restaurants nearby.

As he took a seat and stared out the window, he saw his brothers pull up in their big black Escalade. It was pimped out and trimmed in chrome and stood out as much as the custom license plate, "TRPL ACTION." He chuckled. They used to call one another that as kids when other boys would mess with them. You messed with one Spencer, you messed with all three.

They did most things together, but of course being a deputy after serving in the Navy as a SEAL was Mike's calling. Danny and Jack had the business sense and mind. Plus, they loved living in Chance so much that after college and making it big in Charlotte, they pooled their money and opened up Spencer's dance hall and bar. It was one of the local hot spots. They were thinking of expanding, but there was a lot to consider. With a bigger place came more problems, including people coming in from out of town and getting rowdy. They would need more security, and of course they wanted him to head it all.

The door chimed just as Marlena walked by and placed his ice tea down onto the table. She looked nervous as usual but just as gorgeous with her long blonde hair pulled back and arranged on the top of her head in some fancy style he noticed other women complimented her on. But it was her gorgeous, bold green eyes the color of emeralds that stood out most. They showed so much emotion. When she was excited, happy, sad, and even scared. Like now, the poor woman was shaking.

She tightened up the moment Danny and Jack slid next to her. Jack placed his hand on her waist.

"Afternoon, Marlena. You look real pretty today," he told her.

"Thank you, Jack."

"She sure does. We got lucky snagging you as our waitress. Good job, brother," Danny said to Marlena, keeping his eyes on her and not glancing at Mike at all.

Mike had to chuckle. How many times had he told his brother not to be too flirty or pushy with Marlena? It just set her on further edge. They needed her calm and relaxed, so they could make a move.

She slid to the left, pulling out her pad as she glanced around the diner looking to see where she needed to go next.

"Can I start you with something to drink? Maybe you know what you'd like to order," she said, holding the pen and not making eye contact with Jack or Danny.

"What I want isn't on the menu," Jack said to her. She swung her head at him fast and then held his gaze.

Mike's heart pounded inside of his chest. What were these guys doing?

"And what would that be, Jack?" she asked with a little attitude.

"Can you see if one of my dads can make me a special egg on the burger? He'll know what toppings to add," he told her.

She wrote it down. "Sure thing. How about you guys?" she asked.

Danny leaned back and rubbed his belly. "I want to save room for some dessert," he said and eyed her breasts. They were full and plump, nearly pouring from the blouse she wore. But unlike the other waitress, Alice, Marlena had her blouse buttoned up high. But it still accentuated her large breasts. She was a sexy woman.

"Well then maybe you'd like a salad?" she suggested and Jack laughed. So did Mike.

"I'll take the same thing as Jack," Danny said, sounding a little grumpy.

She then looked at Mike.

"What do you suggest, Marlena? What special is the best today?"

"Well, the chicken cheesesteak with homemade hash browns is most popular today. I don't know how many orders your dads have left."

"Well put me down for that, and if not, then make mine the same as my brothers," he told her. She nodded then walked away, clearing some dishes from another table then placing a bill down on another.

"She works so hard. She's been doing double shifts. Mom said that Tara might not come back," Jack told them.

"Shit, really? Then they should hire someone else. Marlena looks so damn tired all the time," Danny said.

"She's still gorgeous," Mike added, watching her. She ran around that place smiling, talking to the townspeople, making everyone feel so welcome. Yet he couldn't help but think her smiles, her laughter, were all a show. Like she was hurting inside and hiding it. It was just a gut instinct, but he felt it.

"What's that expression for?" Jack asked him.

He looked at his brother. They were all big men. Six feet three, filled with muscles. All in great physical condition. Hell, he was a Navy SEAL. Had his hang-ups of his and insecurities when it came to trust. But Marlena affected him like no one else.

"You know what I'm thinking. Why do you two need to be so forward with her? She's timid and shy, you'll only scare her off."

"Says you. Didn't you see her cheeks blush, and her nipples harden? She's attracted to us, we just need to get through the wall she has up," Danny told him.

"Don't do that. Don't talk all big and bad like getting to know her and making her our woman is so simple and that she'll just accept it. You know as well as I do that she holds back information on herself, doesn't talk about where she came from, nothing. Deciding to engage in a ménage relationship and commit instead of just getting off on sharing is different," Mike said, clenching his teeth and whispering low.

Marlena returned with two ice teas. "You got the last special, Mike. Your dad Regan is making it for you while your dad Roy makes Danny and Jack's special order. It will be a little bit. Can I grab you anything else for now?" she asked.

"We heard that Tara may not be returning to work here. Do you know if our mom and dads are going to hire someone else to help out?" Danny asked her.

"I'm not sure. Alice and I are sharing working double shifts. But she's still in college and trying to take more courses. I think your parents might have to hire someone part-time."

"You work too hard, Marlena. One day off a week doesn't seem like enough," Jack said to her.

"Well, it's not like I can't use the money."

She heard the bell by the front door ring and she looked a bit tired. Mike caught sight of Vicky Reynolds and he exhaled in annoyance.

"I'll go check on your orders," Marlena said and she looked annoyed. Could she be jealous of Vicky Reynolds? Vicky made it pretty clear she was interested in Mike and his brothers, but the three of them weren't biting. Vicky was after their money. She was high-maintenance and a bit stuck-up. Not their type at all.

* * * *

"Good afternoon. Would you like to sit at the counter or do you need a table?" Marlena asked Vicky Reynolds. The woman was dressed up like she was going to some garden tea party in Charlotte. However, she faked her conservative Christian values, especially when it came to men and being pretty promiscuous. She had money, charm, and a way about her that had men drooling or at least giving her their full attention. Truth was, as Mercedes had witnessed, Vicky was nothing more than a Southern slut on the prowl for a rich husband.

Vicky gave her the once-over and scrunched her face as if Marlena smelled or had vomit on her clothes. She was insulting and arrogant. Something Marlena had had enough of years ago back North.

Vicky ignored her and glanced around the diner. She pushed past Marlena, like she had done a time or two before, like she was an object in the way and meaningless. Despite her mind telling her to not be insulted or feel like a nobody, Marlena did. She lowered her eyes and walked back toward another table.

"Hey, sweetie, don't let that prissy witch make you sad. You're way prettier than she is, and have a lot more class and appeal," Johnny Jacobs told her as he took her hand and placed the bill and some money into it.

He and his brother had just finished up lunch. She gave a soft smile.

"Thank you, Johnny. I'm fine. See you again next week?" she asked him, and he winked.

"You betcha. Maybe let Roy and Regan know it would be nice if they put Rita's meatloaf on as a special. Love that woman's cooking," he said and tipped his hat before him and his brother headed out. She walked over to the register and counted the money. Johnny had given her a hefty tip. She smiled. Then glanced toward the table where Mike and his brothers were just as the bell chimed for her to deliver food. She knew it was their order. Vicky stood there, smiling and trying to ease her way onto Danny's lap because there wasn't an additional seat.

"Vicky, cool it, will ya? There's no room for you. Why are you here anyway?" Jack asked her.

Marlena could hear the conversation but tried not to listen as she delivered the food to their table.

"Excuse me," she said, trying to get past Vicky. The woman huffed and puffed as Marlena had to give her a slight bump in order to not drop the platters of food onto the men's laps. When she finished, the men were smiling.

"Can I get you anything else to go along with your lunches?"

"Coffee please, doll," Mike told her and winked.

"Make that three," Jack said and smiled at her. Vicky gave her mean looks and placed her hands on her hips.

"I thought we were going to get together again. Didn't the three of us have a good time at my place last week?" Vicky asked and Marlena was shocked. Hell, she was angry and jealous and she had no reason to be. She hurried away and could hear some heated discussion going on between the men and her, but Marlena didn't care. They were just like men back in New York and North Carolina. They were after one thing and she sure didn't need any of that, and not triple time.

She made the coffees and then hurried to the table to deliver them. She just wanted to get to the other two tables she had now that lunchtime was dying down and the place was emptying out.

"Excuse me," she said as she heard Jack tell Vicky to leave and that they weren't interested in what she was offering.

"But you were interested the other night. Three times," she said.

Marlena was placing the cups down.

"Cool it, Vicky. Your lies don't work with us. You're delusional," Danny told her.

"Me? You know you want a piece of this. Hell, the three of you been sniffing around for months. Now, you can't seriously be blowing me off," she was saying as Marlena was passing the cup of coffee to Jack. She pulled back the tray, noticing the men staring at her, not Vicky.

"Are you kidding me? She's a mouse," Vicky yelled out, slamming down on the tray and sending the hot coffee onto Marlena. As Vicky stormed out, Marlena cried out and bent forward, trying to pull her blouse out to get the hot liquid away from her skin. The men stood up.

"Oh God, Marlena," Jack yelled out.

"Here grab the cloth, some cold water quickly," Danny said and Marlena pushed his hand away. She could feel her skin burning. She felt the tears reach her eyes. She needed to get this blouse off. The place erupted in chaos and she was embarrassed, in pain, and angry. She pulled away and hurried behind the counter, passing a concerned Roy and then Regan as she headed to the side bathroom. She closed the door and unbuttoned her blouse, pulling it open. Her skin was bright red along her ribs and belly. She felt the tears in her eyes and with shaking hands turned on the faucet.

The door opened and there was Mike. She pulled her blouse over her bra, covering her breasts.

"Go away. I'm fine. I've got this," she said and scrunched her eyes together as her skin felt on fire.

"I can't believe she did that. I swear that woman is an idiot. Let me take a look, Marlena. I know first aid. I know about burns."

She shook her head as Rita came in.

"Here's the first aid kit and some burn cream."

"I'm okay, Rita. Just give me a minute and I'll finish up the last tables."

"Don't be silly. You let Mike check out that burn and get some burn cream on it. While I take care of the tables and Roy calms down Danny and Jack."

"Please tell them it's okay. I'll be fine," she said and felt the tears on her eyelashes.

Rita left the bathroom and Mike stepped closer. "Let me see the damage."

She lifted her blouse, holding it against her breasts so he couldn't see.

He held her gaze and licked his lower lip. He took a deep breath and then looked down. His face scrunched up and he knelt down lower.

"Son of a bitch. This is going to blister. That stupid bitch. I swear that woman needs a swift kick in her ass."

"You sound like you don't like her."

He looked upward, locking gazes with Marlena, then opened up the first aid kit. He looked so huge kneeling down in the small bathroom and in full uniform. He was big, tall, and so very handsome. She felt her belly flutter and certain parts come to life being this close to him. She swallowed hard. She didn't need any trouble. She had enough back in Connecticut.

"Who said I like her? My brothers and I can't stand her."

"Then why did you sleep with—"

She bit her lip and stopped from talking.

She felt Mike's hands on her hips and then he gave them a squeeze. She looked at him.

"Don't believe everything you hear, darling. People lie all the time."

"You don't have to tell me," she replied, staring at him.

"Lift that blouse higher. This is going to sting a bit. I just want to wash my hands to ensure that they're clean."

He stood up and squeezed next to her to wash his hands with soap and water in the sink. He reached past her, brushing slightly against her breasts and the blouse she held in a death grip against her body.

"I can do this, Mike. You should go back to enjoy lunch with your brothers." He stepped in front of her, lowering his eyes as if peeking at the gap to check out her cleavage. She wanted him, too. The thought surprised her.

"Let's get something straight, Marlena. You are our number-one concern. You're too beautiful, too sweet to have to feel any pain. What Vicky did was unacceptable and downright mean. She'll pay for it. Now let me take care of you."

She swallowed hard and nodded her head.

"Good girl," he whispered. Those blue eyes held hers and damn it did her pussy just leak some serious cream. The man was so sexy he should be illegal.

She held her breath as he prepared to place some burn cream onto her ribs and belly. His hard thick fingers caressed softly.

He paused a moment. "What's this?" he asked. She swallowed hard. She didn't have to look down. The hip-hugger black dress pants she wore revealed her hips and the scar from the burn she got from the fire Peter set.

"It's nothing. I've had it for a long time," she told him.

"You've gotten burned before?" he questioned.

"Hazards of being a waitress, I guess." She lied and looked away from him. He didn't need to know the truth. No one did. It was bad enough she allowed Peter to control her life, her every move. She didn't have to reveal how stupid and gullible she had been. The older, sexy man with charm and power turned her world upside down and then lost all control and tried to kill her. Yeah, she definitely needed to keep that to herself.

She swallowed hard. She took quick breaths as he spoke to her and eased her pain.

"That's it, nice and easy breaths, I'm almost through. You're very strong, Marlena."

The door opened and she gasped then closed her eyes. Danny and Jack were there.

"Are you okay? Is it bad?" Jack asked.

"I'm applying some burn cream. Hopefully it doesn't blister," Mike said.

She opened her eyes and locked gazes with Jack. His blue eyes held hers then his eyes swept over her breasts.

There was no way the two of them could fit into the small bathroom with her and Mike.

"I'll be fine. Don't worry. Please just go finish eating," she said to them as Mike pulled back.

"I'm going to apply some gauze to place over the cream. It might be smart to go see Dr. Anders."

She shook her head. "I'm fine, Mike. Really. It's just a burn," she said, and in her mind she had flashbacks of Peter, and how he torched her apartment in anger and how she nearly died in the fire. She shivered.

Marlena felt the hand on her waist then another hand take her hand.

She opened her eyes. Mike's hand lay half over her hip and ass. Jack's held her hand.

"Are you okay? That coffee was piping hot."

She nodded her head and pulled her hand from his.

"Please, go back out there to eat. I feel terrible for ruining your lunch."

"Ruining our lunch? That wasn't your fault, that was Vicky's," Danny said from behind Jack.

"Just go. Please," she said and tried stepping away from Mike.

"Let me tape this last side so the gauze stays in place. He unrolled the tape and added it to the bandage and against her skin. He stood up and she held the blouse against her chest. Mike stared at her.

"You sure that you're okay?"

She nodded her head. "Go. Please," she whispered.

He nodded his head and Jack and Danny walked out. She felt badly and as Mike began to leave she reached out and touched his arm. The contact burned, she was so attracted to the man. To his cologne, his muscles, his compassion.

"Thank you, Mike," she said, and he gave a soft smile, nodded his head, and walked out of the room. The door closed and she turned around to look into the mirror. She was shocked to see how flush she was, how her eyes sparkled, and her body hummed with an awareness. She looked at the bandage, almost feeling his fingers gentle against her skin again. She couldn't trust him or his brothers. She couldn't trust any man. They could be just like Peter.

She felt the tears sting her eyes as she washed the coffee from her blouse, wrung it out, then used the air dryer on the wall to try and dry it a little. Then she put it back on and thought about Vicky and what she'd said. She'd said they spent time together and that they enjoyed one another's company at her place last week. Could it be true? Could they not be as kind, and caring as they seem to be to Marlena? What if they slept with Vicky and now ignored her and pretended they never did? They were men who used women for what they wanted. She already experienced that once before, and look what it cost her. The fear had her forcing the thoughts from her head as well as any attraction to Mike, Danny, and Jack. She didn't need more pain. She had a lifetime full already.

Chapter 2

"Her friends are here but she's not. Do you think she's in pain from that burn today at the diner?" Danny asked Jack as they stood by the bar in Spencer's.

"Probably, although she rarely goes out," Jack replied, his eyes on Marlena's friends, who all looked like they were uncomfortable and not having fun. It was strange, but the three women were all stunning, yet they didn't date or seem to be interested in doing so. He had to laugh. His good friends Will, Leo, and Hank Ferguson from Ferguson construction were very protective of their personal assistant Adele. By the way they talked about her, he'd say they were interested in getting to know Adele outside of work. But Adele was a lot like Marlena. She was shy, reserved, didn't give much info on herself, and was a hard worker. She was an overachiever like Marlena.

"Mike got off work at five and saw Marlena heading out of the diner. He said that Mom said Marlena was in pain and that she told Marlena if she didn't think she could work tomorrow, to let her know tonight. I doubt she'll call in sick," Danny said to his brother.

"I doubt it, too. She's not a quitter, or at least doesn't seem like one. Damn, I'm still so pissed off at Vicky. She's such a troublemaker," Jack said.

"I know she is. You never should have fooled around with her."

"I was drunk, bro. What the fuck. It's not like I slept with her," Danny stated in annoyance.

"No, you didn't. I could only imagine what type of stalker she would be."

Danny chuckled. "We'd probably have to call in some favors or get Mike to pull one of his Navy SEAL moves."

Jack laughed.

They were both quiet a moment. Danny thought about Marlena. She was so beautiful, with long blonde hair and those bright green eyes. She was young, too. Twenty-three, he thought his mom mentioned. Eight years younger than Mike, who was the youngest. She had an amazing body, too, but she didn't flaunt it. Instead she covered it up and tried to hide her beauty. It often made him wonder why.

"I can't stop thinking about her, Danny," Jack said then took a slug of beer from a bottle.

"I know what you mean. Neither can I. Especially after today. She looked so insulted and scared. God, when we walked into that bathroom and I saw her body, holy shit," Danny said and ran his fingers through his hair.

"I know. I felt like my heart was in my throat. She's sexy and voluptuous. It makes me feel protective and possessive of her, especially after what Vicky did."

"I hear ya. It's the same here. I just can't help but to wonder about her and why she's so secretive."

"Jack, what do you think about what Mike told us? You know, about the scar on her hip. He thinks it was a burn."

"It could be anything. What are you thinking?" Danny asked while he played with an empty glass of whisky.

"I don't know. Like she might have had a hard life. Like maybe someone hurt her and that's why she's so quiet," Jack replied.

"Well, when we get to know her, and she finally lets her guard down, maybe we can ask her about that scar, and why she held back."

Jack chuckled. "You sound pretty confident that she'll let us into her life."

"She's the first woman in a while that the three of us are attracted to. We've talked about sharing a woman and making that commitment for years. We're older than her, we're tired of messing around. We look at her and think of all the things Mom had with our dads. I'm ready," Danny admitted.

They heard some laughter and turned to look at the large crowd of people who showed up. There was Vicky, her arm wrapped around some idiot's arm as she hugged it and smiled. They looked half in the bag already, and Danny wondered why the bouncers even let them in.

"Looks like trouble if you ask me," Jack said, nodding toward one of the security guys nearby. He nodded back, spoke into his wrist mic, and Danny knew that they would all keep an extra eye on this crew. But it didn't take long for trouble to brew. Vicky gave them the evil eye and then whispered to the bozo whose arm she was hugging. The pompous ass looked straight at Danny and Jack, and Jack smiled.

"Let me get this one. You got the last asshole."

Danny chuckled.

"There are more of them than you. Let our security handle it."

"What? And miss the look on that bitch's face when we send her and her entourage of shit on their asses out the front door? No can do, bro. Her stinking reputation is going to get more ruined than it already is. She'll never step into this place again," Jack said and stood up from the stool. He turned his back on the crowd.

"Not so smart. That guy is bigger than you and he's drunk. He'll think nothing of—"

"Hey, assholes. I've got a bone to pick with you." The guy approached from behind and Danny slightly turned on his stool.

Jack chuckled.

The guy pressed a finger into Jack's back. In a flash, Jack had the guy's finger bent backward and the man kneeling on the floor crying out in pain.

"Hey, asshole, you don't belong here and neither does that trash. You're going to leave our fine establishment right now in one piece or in multiple pieces. Your choice."

"You're such an asshole, Jack. You'd pick that low-class waitress over me? Your loss," Vicky said from behind him.

Jack looked her over.

"I don't think so. Take your slutty, disgusting, unladylike self out of our place now and don't ever return. You and your friends aren't allowed here."

"What? You can't do that," she yelled as the security guys grabbed the one guy on the floor and another took Vicky by her upper arm.

"Yes, ma'am, he can. They own the place. They can do whatever they want," the bouncer told her and started directing her toward the front door.

"You'll be sorry and so will the ugly bitch waitress. I hope I scarred her today," she spat out, and Jack started walking toward her all pissed off, but Danny grabbed his arm and pressed up against his side.

"She isn't worth it. We'll protect Marlena from her. She's just making idle threats."

Danny and Jack turned around but not before Danny locked gazes with Marlena's friend Adele. He nodded at her and she pulled her bottom lip between her teeth and looked at her friends. They had to have heard the whole episode. They would probably tell Marlena. He realized that he didn't care. She was going to find out sooner or later that they planned on making her their woman. Why not through the grapevine, first?

* * * *

Marlena changed the bandage on her stomach and ribs. She applied some ointment in hopes that it wouldn't scar. It was bad enough she had the scar on her hipbone from the fire back in Connecticut.

She pulled the tank top back into place and adjusted her breasts in the cups of her bra. She needed to go shopping for more clothes. What she had was getting dingy-looking. She had saved enough working at the diner, but she wished she had the forty thousand dollars that was in her savings account back in Connecticut. She couldn't contact anyone there. There was no one to trust to help her close out the account and have the money transferred to an account here. Besides, she didn't want to give Peter the chance to find her and come after her again.

Like Detective Morgan had explained to her, no evidence was found to prove that Peter started the fire. He had an alibi, another woman who swore that he was with her. There was nothing she could do. She knew that Peter lied. She knew the other woman lied for him because Peter was a manipulative bastard with money. Marlena had nothing. No family, no one to trust, not even Detective Morgan, who told her to disappear, and that it was the best thing she could do because he couldn't find any evidence to stick to Peter. When Marlena suggested that she leave town, he didn't try to stop her. In fact, he agreed that it would be a good idea. He promised to keep the investigation open and push for more evidence, and she believed him. It was that or wait for Peter to strike again and next time be successful in killing her.

She shivered from the thought as she slipped her feet into her flip-flops and headed toward the small porch. This was a nice little cottage. She rented it from Rita Spencer's brother, who owned a large piece of land by a lake. His house was a good distance from the cottage, so she had lots of privacy.

She let the screen door slam closed behind her and inhaled the later morning air. It was a beautiful Sunday, and so different from Connecticut. She'd lived in an apartment, where people came and went saying hello and have a nice day, but not much more. She made a few friends, but when she met Peter he took full control of her social schedule. The only time she was at peace was at work in the accounting office where she worked as a CPA. She was moving up in the firm, enjoying making good money, dressing nicely, and being able to establish a career and a future. She never thought that accepting a date with the wealthy entrepreneur, Peter Jones, would have changed her destiny entirely.

She took a deep breath and released it as she walked down the steps taking a leisurely stroll through the backyard and toward the lake. There was a nice bench and some picnic tables there that Rita's brother and family used years ago. His kids were all grown up now and living elsewhere. Two in town and one in North Carolina.

She loved how calm and peaceful it was out here. She remembered showing up, not knowing anything about Chance except for its name. She figured it meant something. Perhaps to take a chance and stay in the town, find a job, and settle down for a while, putting the past behind her. She figured it was fate that first day she started looking for work and met Rita Spencer. She was so kind, and they hit it off immediately. She had a real motherly way about her. She was envious of her sons. She wondered if Mike, Danny, and Jack knew just how good they had it having parents to love them. Heck, they even had two dads. That was shocking at first, but soon became so interesting and natural. She learned fast about the ménage relationships and about the commitment. It was pretty magical to watch.

She thought about the look of the town. Not old or rundown, very clean, well maintained, and freshly painted, and it all coordinated. There was just about every kind of store she would need and even some she didn't. Like the hardware store, the lingerie store, and the cigar store. She smiled. She could spend the day just walking the two blocks of stores, saying hello to other local people and discussing the weather, the change of the seasons, or how rabbits and deer repeatedly destroyed Mrs. Ulster's gardens.

She smiled. It was all so normal. Like a different world than what she came from.

She got to the bench and took a seat. Her belly ached a little but she ignored it and watched the water. This was peaceful. This was where nothing else mattered and everything was simple. She embraced it.

She closed her eyes after a while, feeling pretty tired from the long workweek. As she was just about to doze off, she thought she heard her name. She ignored it. The pull to take a little catnap under the large tree was too inviting. But then she heard it again, and this time she recognized the voice. *Danny Spencer. Oh shit.*

She sat up too quickly and cringed from the ache. Danny was at her side a moment later and kneeling by the bench.

"Whoa, slow down, Marlena. Are you still sore from the burn?" he asked, placing his hand on her bare knee.

She pushed a strand of hair behind her ear and looked up at him.

"What are you doing here?" she asked.

"Checking on our girl. What do you think?" he asked and caressed her knee. He looked her over, let his eyes roam over her chest and then to her lips.

"You look relaxed, and a lot different than the uniform our mom has you wear."

"Yeah well it's hard to keep a white button-down blouse clean, and these flip flops wouldn't work so well with all the walking I do at work. My feet would be covered with blisters by the end of the day."

She sat up straighter and Danny stood up then took a seat next to her.

"God, it's so beautiful out here. It hasn't changed much at all," he said, looking out at the water.

She watched him. Danny was very attractive, and had lighter hair than Mike. Jack's was almost blond where Danny's was a light brown. Mike's was dark brown, but the three of them shared the same gorgeous blue eyes.

He wore a pair of blue jeans, cowboy boots, and a tight-fitting light blue shirt. She could smell his cologne. It was something simple and not fancy or overwhelming. It made her want to inhale to get a better scent of it. She crossed her legs and then placed her hands on her lap. They both stared out at the water.

"My brothers, cousins, and I had a lot of good times out here."

"Really? You swam in that lake? It's safe?" she asked. He chuckled as he looked at her. *God, he's so handsome.* She had to turn away. She felt the warning signs creep up and down her spine. Men couldn't be trusted. Men wanted to hurt, to manipulate and control a woman. Even the ones who seemed so nice.

"It's safe, darling. There's even a natural spring that runs through there. But don't go in there by yourself," he warned.

"Why not?" she asked, feeling concerned.

"It's pretty deep in the center. It's not smart to swim alone."

"I would only go in to my waist. I don't know how to swim," she said then stood up from the bench.

"Then definitely not alone. I could teach you how to swim," he said, standing up and placing his hand on her hips.

She shook her head and stepped back. "That's okay. No need to learn. I won't go in," she said and walked around the bench to try and put some distance between them. If felt good to have his hands on her waist. To have him act as though he cared and wanted to teach her to swim. But she knew what he was after. She wasn't interested.

"Marlena, do my brothers and I scare you?" he asked her. She was shocked as she looked up and locked gazes with him.

"Scare me? Why would you ask that?" she asked. He remained where he was standing. The light from the sun cascaded around him, making him appear almost spiritual, like some savior. Her savior? She shook the thoughts from her head.

"Darling, you get this look sometimes that clearly displays an emotion of fear. It concerns my brothers and me. What could we do to show you that we can be trusted?"

She ran her hand along the top of the bench and looked away from him.

"I'm sorry, Danny. I think you should go. It's my day off and I'd like to relax and be alone."

"Marlena, I'll do as you wish. I came by to check on that burn and make sure it was healing okay."

"It's fine. I even changed the bandage," she replied.

"Good. You take care of that and make sure it doesn't get worse. You're not working tomorrow, are you?"

"Of course I am."

He stepped closer to her.

"You should be resting. That burn is going to ache a bunch working all day the way you do."

"I have to work. I wouldn't leave your mom and dads hanging, Danny. There are no replacements, yet," she said.

"You're not replaceable, Marlena. You're perfect," he said, and she felt her cheeks warm. She lowered her eyes and a moment later Danny was next to her. He touched her hand, bringing it to his lips.

"You enjoy your day off. Maybe after this week, you'll accept my offer to teach you how to swim. I'm sure Mike and Jack would love to teach you, too." He kissed her knuckles, winked, and then released her hand and walked away. She followed him with her eyes as he headed own the path and to the side of her house. She saw the red pickup truck. Different than that Escalade he and Jack always drove.

She released a long breath and closed her eyes.

He was just as handsome and likable as Mike and Jack. But she just couldn't risk getting fooled again. She couldn't. Besides, Peter would always be a concern she'd have. He had to screw up somewhere. He would get busted for the crimes he committed, and for what he tried to do to her. He had to, or she would never truly rest or settle down anywhere. The fear would be overwhelming.

Chapter 3

"So what are you going to do?" Alicia asked Marlena as Adele and Mercedes grabbed wine glasses and a bottle of wine.

They had all come over to Marlena's house for Sunday dinner and to enjoy some time together. Plus Alicia was dying to talk to Marlena about Mike, Danny, and Jack and what she missed by not going to Spencer's.

"I'm not going to do anything. I told you guys. I'm not getting involved with any men. I'm not ready," she told them as she tucked her feet under her as Mercedes handed her a glass of Chardonnay.

"You are out of your mind. Deputy Spencer is so hot. The women go crazy over him. But then again, this sheriff's department, from the man himself down to ranks in his command, is gorgeous. They're also experienced and tough. Most of them were in the service. That in itself is sexy," Mercedes said.

"That's not what I need right now. These guys can get any woman they want. They more than likely have had their share of women, and might I point out are much older than I am. The last thing I need are three men trying to command my life and then lose it on me," Marlena said and then took a sip of wine.

"Marlena, I know I'm the last person to stand here and give you a pep-talk about trusting men. I've declined offers of dates out of fear of getting hurt again. We've all had similar experiences from our pasts where we got hurt, or were even betrayed." Adel swallowed hard and looked at the others then back at Marlena.

"But I have to tell you, the way Danny and Jack looked the other night, the way they talked about you and stood up for you when

Vicky was spewing venom, wasn't any bullshit. They like you. They care about you," Adele told her.

"Hell, Mike spent more than his allotted lunchtime at the diner taking care of you when you got burned. He was late for a meeting with Sheriff Gordon, and that just doesn't happen. But when he got back to the department and told him what happened, the sheriff was pissed off, too. Called me into his office to ask me to keep him posted on your healing," Mercedes told her.

"Sheriff Gordon? Why would he do that?" Marlena asked.

"Because that's how this town works," Alicia whispered in her normal shy tone, appearing timid despite being here amongst friends. She was lacking in self-confidence despite how smart and beautiful she was, all because of a man.

"You know we're being watched over by all the men in town. It's for our protection. Don't you feel it? The way whenever something seems to go wrong someone is around to help. There had to be a crowd of men wanting to help you at the diner when Vicky knocked that hot coffee onto you," Alicia said.

Marlena nodded her head and laid her hand gently over her belly.

"It hurt so badly. I wanted to rip my blouse from my body but I felt someone undo my apron as I bent forward trying to pull the material from my skin. Danny, Mike, and Jack were around me but it wasn't them. Now that I think about it, in all that chaos there were mostly men in the diner and a few women. It hurt so badly. I'm not really sure," Marlena said and then looked at Mercedes, who smiled.

"Chance is different than any other town. We each found it, and found one another because it's so special here. If you're not ready to open up your heart to Mike, Danny, and Jack, because you're not attracted to them, then so be it. But if it's just because you're scared of getting hurt, then it's wrong. It's not fair. What that guy did to you to hurt you back in Connecticut is in the past and you can't let him ruin your future. I've seen how Jack, Danny, and Mike look at you.

They care. They want to protect you, hell, they could already love you," Mercedes told her.

"Me?" Marlena asked and the tears filled her eyes. They could all see it.

"Who couldn't love you? You're smart, beautiful, strong, and a great friend. Besides, if for some strange reason we're all wrong and they do hurt you, the three of us will kick their asses," Adele stated firmly. Alicia covered her mouth and laughed.

Mercedes made a fist. "Hell yeah."

Adele reached over and covered Marlena's knee. "You take your time, and you be sure. This type of relationship is way different then the norm. It's intense, it's heavy, and involves a major commitment on all ends."

"Great, just scare the crap out of her, Adele," Mercedes stated and took a sip of wine.

"What? It's not like I mentioned the sex and having three men as lovers means all holes are open game for cock."

"Adele!"

Alicia gasped and gave Adele's leg a slap.

They all started laughing.

"Oh God, I don't think I could ever do any of that," Marlena said softly.

"Honey, with men like that who adore you, who want to protect you, care for you, and be your everything, the fear won't matter. In a ménage relationship, the men cater to the woman's every need. It ensures she is never alone or uncared for, and always protected and cherished. Haven't you noticed the expressions of love, of satisfaction and contentedness on people's faces around here who are involved in ménage relationships? The women are simply glowing and the men very possessive and caring. It's magical," Mercedes whispered then took a sip of wine.

"Sounds like you want that, too," Alicia whispered.

"I think we all could use some catering to. Some men to take care of us, love us, and obsess over us after all we've gone through in our pasts. Will it happen? Will we each meet the perfect men and maybe fall in love? Who the hell knows? But if you asked me right now, if you dared me to take a shot at the possibility of finding true love in multiple men together, hell yeah I'd take that dare. I'd give this love thing a shot, and if it's wrong, if I get hurt, then so be it. Life is way too short to not take chances. Besides, I'm not getting any younger," Adele stated.

They all nodded their heads and Mercedes raised her wine glass.

"To finding true love, ménage style in Chance."

They all clinked glasses.

"God help us. I just don't want to feel pain, feel heartache ever again," Marlena said and they all mumbled in agreement and sat back enjoying their wine, their friendship, and the hope that Chance brought them happiness once and for all.

Chapter 4

Peter Jones sat in the van overlooking the water. His hands were shaking. Looking down, he saw the swollen knuckles, the scrapes and the blood. He was losing his mind. He was obsessed with her.

He reached across the seat and pulled the picture and frame in front of him. He leaned it on the steering wheel and stared into her green eyes. The eyes of innocence. That was until he got a hold of her. Marlena had become his everything, yet he made her feel worthless one minute and placed her on a pedestal the next.

He had always been indecisive. To point that it drove his father crazy. And his mother suffered. But unlike Marlena, his mother was mouthy and obnoxious and his father gave it to her good.

Peter tightened the hold on the frame. He stared at the picture of him and Marlena on the boat. She looked angelic, pure, sweet. That was why he had sex with other women, smacked them around and tied them up, because his Marlena was too good for that.

He wanted to keep her pure. To keep her as his woman. He thought she would accept his needs and desires without explanation.

That same night as the boat ride, he embarrassed her. Made her cry and feel worthless and then he made her stay with him and pleasure him. He created her. He turned her into the woman he needed her to be in order for him to keep control of his real emotions and to hide what he was really like. A monster of sorts. A man living two separate lives. A womanizer, a batterer, a man who needed constant control of life and death. His violent behavior was getting worse. He enjoyed destroying things, burning things, and breaking things. Especially finding the weakness within them. He went too far with the fire. He was caught up in a phrase, an idea in his head that told him if he burned her to death then she would no longer have a hold of his heart. She would perish and so would the connections he had with her. But she lived. She fought and survived and he failed.

He ground his teeth.

He pushed her too far. She left him, and instead of trying to make things up to her and gain control of this out of control feelings he had, he decided to kill her. He tried to stay away. He tried fucking others. Nothing worked.

He was losing his focus at work. His edge was gone and it was all Marlena's fault.

She turned out to be just like his mother after all. She made him try to kill her.

Months had passed. Months. And here he was, sitting in a van, planning his next move and knowing the game had changed. He wanted Marlena back. She proved how strong she was and how special. He would find her and bring her back to him. As long as she were faithful, he would keep her alive.

He ran a finger along her picture. He brought his fingertips to his lips and touched them back against her picture. He saw the blood, the swollen knuckles, and he felt aroused, and in need. "I'm coming for you, Marlena. You belong to me always. I'm coming."

* * * *

Jack and his brothers had the day off. They came through the back door of the diner to see their parents as the breakfast crowd simmered down. His thoughts were on Marlena, and the burn she had sustained on Friday, as well as how she reacted to his brother Danny on Sunday. Danny felt that she was afraid of him, perhaps men in general, and it made them all think that someone hurt her.

"Hey, this is a nice surprise. Nothing better to do on your days off?" their mom asked and gave them each a hug and kiss hello.

"Nah, they're looking to fill their bellies," Roy chimed in as he flipped some burgers on the large grill.

"Or maybe they came to see a particular waitress they seem very concerned over," Regan added and Jack was too busy looking around for Marlena. He could see the back of her hair as she lifted a large amount of plates and began carrying them into the kitchen.

She caught sight of him and his brothers and nearly dropped the dishes.

"Marlena, you shouldn't be lifting all those dishes at once. Not with your side aching the way it is." Their mom reprimanded her as she took the dishes and began placing them into the sudsy sink water.

"I'm fine, Mrs. Spencer. Really," she said and used her forearm to wipe her brow then she turned and headed back out.

Jack looked at his brothers, and they both appeared concerned.

"Mom, is she really hurting from the burn?" Danny asked her.

Their mom took a deep breath and released it. "It's blistered up real good. Don't know how she's avoiding banging into anything that could pop them. I hope Vicky doesn't set her feet in here or I may have to kick her out myself," their mom said as she scrubbed the dishes.

"Maybe we should talk to her, and have Dr. Anders stop in to take a peek," Danny suggested.

"Now, son, I know you and your brothers are concerned considering you were here when she got burned and caused the confrontation, but she's a grown woman who likes to keep to herself. Respect that," Regan said to them.

"We didn't cause Vicky to do that," Danny said.

"You don't think so? Marlena is a very attractive young woman. She turns down men's offers left and right for dates around here. So when a piece of jealous trash like Vicky comes sniffing around and sees competition, the nails come out. Poor Marlena hadn't a clue it was coming," their mom said, and it sounded like she was warning them to stay clear. Like maybe she thought her own sons weren't good enough for Marlena.

Marlena entered the kitchen, posting two more orders up onto the rack that displayed the orders that needed to be made.

She cringed when she reached up and then she took a deep breath. Before any of them could say anything to her, she disappeared back out into the diner.

Jack went up to their mom. He wrapped his arms around her waist and placed his head on her shoulder. "Now, Mom, you telling us you don't think your own sons are good enough for Marlena?"

She swung her head toward him.

"Jack Montgomery Spencer, you dare hurt that girl or break her heart, I swear I'll take a rolling pin to that hard head of yours."

"Mom, come on. Have you ever seen the three of us like the same woman? Ever see us interested in a woman at the same time?" Jack asked.

She looked at Roy and Regan, who shrugged their shoulders.

"That's what I thought," Jack said, releasing her then grabbing a fresh piece of carrot off the counter.

"Jack, I'm warning you and your brothers. She's special. She's sweet and I like her."

"So do we," Danny said as he leaned against the doorframe, arms crossed and staring at their mom.

She peeked through the divider where the food went up.

"Then you'd better get out there and make your intentions known, 'cause Deputy Taylor Dawn is out there with two of his brothers, and they've been eyeing over Marlena for a week."

* * * *

Marlena was feeling her side burn. She was pretty sure she burst one of the blisters if not all of them that were on her side. She wanted to cry it hurt so bad, but she knew it wasn't as bad as a real burn. When that happened she could hardly breathe through the pain.

She was avoiding the kitchen best she could and was glad she only had two tables left. But then Deputy Taylor Dawn and his two brothers Kurt and Warner arrived. Taylor was in uniform and looking good as usual. Her friends were right, the majority if not all the law enforcement in town were attractive. His brothers were very good-looking, too, but kind of rough and rugged. They had looks in their eyes that warned people to make smart choices. She smiled wide as she greeted them.

"Good afternoon, gentleman, how are ya today?" she asked.

"We're doing good, Marlena, how are you?" Taylor asked her.

"I'm good, thanks. Can I start you off with something to drink?" she asked. They gave her their drink orders but Kurt seemed preoccupied or like he was looking for someone.

"Is everything okay, Kurt?" she asked him.

"Oh yeah, doll, just wondering if your friend Mercedes was around. Sheriff said she was headed here for an early lunch. He's got a meeting and needs her help in an hour."

"Oh, no, Mercedes doesn't usually come here for lunch. She loves enjoying lunch down by the lake in the park by the table behind the gazebo. It's her favorite place to go to relax. So do you need a few more minutes or are you ready to order?" she asked.

Kurt and his brothers seemed disappointed.

"I think we're ready, honey," Warner said to her. She noticed their eyes whisk at something behind her but then back at her again. Their personalities changed a little. They went from being interested in Mercedes and finding out where she was to looking her over and smiling a bunch. They gave their lunch orders and then Taylor leaned back and held her gaze.

"We never see you out at any of the local spots. Where do you like to hang out, Marlena?" he asked.

She felt a bit nervous and wondered why he was asking. She thought these men were interested in Mercedes. Maybe they weren't. But then she felt the hand on her shoulder and at the same time that she flinched, she turned and saw Mike and inhaled his familiar scent.

"Well if it isn't the Dawn brothers. Are they treating my girl okay, or do you need me to put them in their places, Marlena?" Mike asked. She was shocked at him calling her his girl in front of these local men. She also felt a bit of fluttering in her belly like she enjoyed the sound of being his girl. But she needed to remind herself that she wasn't his girl. She didn't belong to anyone.

"What the heck are you doing here on your days off?" Warner asked as he stood up from the table. That was when she realized Jack and Danny were there, too. She felt her belly tighten and her body begin to shake.

"If you'll excuse me, please, I'll get this order in for you gentleman and get the drinks right out to ya."

"No problem, honey. You take your sweet time," Kurt said and winked at her.

She felt Mike squeeze her shoulder. "We'll grab the table in the back corner and wait for you," he whispered. She turned around to hurry to the kitchen to put in the food order then to make the drinks.

"Ain't never seen those three look so pissed off before. When were you going to tell me that you snagged those three sexy Gods?" Alice, the other waitress, asked her. Marlena was shocked. She felt embarrassed as she glanced up to see Rita looking as well as Roy and Reagan.

"I didn't snag up anyone. I don't know what you're talking about," she said to Alice. Then she turned around to make the ice teas for the men.

"Honey, not only do they like you, but they're making their claim, setting down the perimeters, and enforcing their territory."

"What in God's name are you talking about? I don't hardly know them. I'm not interested. I just want to be left alone," she said and then headed out toward the diner. She nearly dropped the one glass of ice tea and she saw Kurt's hands go up as if surrendering and Jack warning him about staying away. Her belly did a series of flips and flops as she approached. Could the Spencer men seriously be threatening the Dawn men over her? No way. She needed to set them all straight.

Danny and Mike were already headed to the corner table, and when she went to place down the ice teas, Jack remained there.

"Those burgers will be out soon," she told them.

"Thanks, Marlena," Kurt said and glanced at Jack. She felt Jack place his hand on her shoulder.

"Come on, baby, come over to our table so we can talk," he said.

She maneuvered her shoulder out of his hand.

"Don't do that, Jack. Please don't call me such things. Are you guys here to eat or what?"

"A little of both," he said and winked. They headed toward the corner table.

Marlena exhaled.

The Dawn brothers chuckled and Jack seemed angry.

She wasn't certain what was going on. She didn't get men. She just didn't understand them. The old Marlena thought every man and woman was nice, truthful, and ready to help. She learned quickly that women could be backstabbers, and men were manipulative and only cared about what they wanted. She'd had the heck scared out of her and nearly died. It made her question people's sincerity and their offers. It all confused her. Trying to figure out what were word games, or who may or may not be telling the truth. It was a damn miracle she let Adele, Alicia, and Mercedes into her life.

She suddenly felt on edge as she headed over to the Spencer men's table. Why did they have to be so damn good-looking? So tall, muscular, and just downright incredible. They even smelled good, and those damn blue eyes of theirs did a number on her body. Why couldn't she just tell them to leave her alone? Maybe ignoring their advances might work for a while, until she figured out how to handle them.

"Can I get you something to drink?" she asked Danny and Mike as Jack sat down at the table.

"Hello to you, too, Marlena," Mike said and held her gaze.

She felt a twinge of guilt. She was never bitchy, even when she had every damn right to be.

She took a deep breath as she looked away and exhaled. No one else came into the diner yet to sit in her section. She would be caught between the Dawn brothers and the Spencer brothers. Just her luck.

"Hello, Deputy Spencer, what can I get you?" she asked.

"First things first, call me Mike. Drop the formalities, Marlena, we've known one another too long to play that game," he said fiercely. She'd insulted him. She could tell and she went to apologize then bit her lip.

"I don't play games. Now would you like to order drinks and something to eat, or are you just coming in here to waste my time and mess with your buddies over there?" she asked without even thinking first.

"Hot damn, Marlena, you are darn sexy when you're all fired up," Jack said to her and Danny gave his brother a hard nudge. She gasped, felt her cheeks turn hot, and she glanced around, hoping no one heard them. But practically everyone in earshot did. She placed her hand on her hip.

"Drinks or no drinks, Mr., Mr., and Mr. Spencer."

They looked shocked, and that nearly made her smile. She'd never seen these men get un-composed or appear like they weren't in charge and setting the pace. She held her ground. Mike held her gaze but spoke to his brothers.

"Danny, you done pissed Marlena off, and that's not our intention coming here to see her. We missed you, Marlena. We were concerned over the blisters and hoping you were healing well."

"I can take care of myself, Dep—Mike. So no need to worry."

She almost called him deputy again but Mike raised one of his eyebrows up at her in challenge and she immediately pulled back. It turned her on that he had that control of her body and her mouth just from his sexy expression. But that also angered her. She was a fool, a sucker for a good sexy cowboy and law enforcement man. He wasn't even wearing that sexy deputy uniform. Instead he had a tight shirt on that revealed his bulging muscles and rock-solid chest in a blue color that accentuated his eyes.

He smirked and she realized she had been staring at him, probably drooling, when the bell rang for an order pickup.

She tried to recover from her actions. "I'll just grab you the usual drinks. Maybe by the time I get back, you'll be ready to order," she said and turned around to head toward the kitchen. She heard the long whistle from Jack as if again she shocked them by her comeback. It was funny, but she enjoyed the little back-and-forth word games with them. It made her belly do flip-flops and her mind wonder if she could let her guard down a little and get to know them better, as friends. But then she felt the fear as she picked up the order for the Dawn brothers. Men were after one thing only and she wasn't ready to lose her heart, her soul and her newfound spirit of determination to make it on her own. No matter how good they smelled, how sexy they were, or how all three of the Spencer brothers turned her on and made her pussy cream just from a little back-and-forth banter. No way.

* * * *

"You have got to pull it together. She needs to be persuaded to get to know us. Maybe try the friends first thing we talked about?" Danny suggested.

"Are you kidding me? Friends first? I've never been friends with a woman first. How the fuck is that even possible with Marlena when every time I see her I fucking feel out of control and possessive? She's too damn sweet and sexy to be a friend," Jack whispered.

"Hell, Danny, I don't think the kind of thoughts a friend has about another friend when I look at Marlena. I saw fucking red when I thought Taylor, Kurt, and Warner were hitting on her," Mike added.

"But they were messing with us. We got that straightened out quickly," Danny added as Marlena set down the lunches for the Dawn brothers and then went back to the counter to pick up the drink orders for them.

She returned, placing down three ice teas with lemon in front of them. Danny inhaled her perfume and then took in the sight of her gorgeous green eyes. She cringed as she reached across the table.

"Sweetie, how is the burn, really?" he asked her and took her hand after she placed the last ice tea down onto the table. She pulled slightly but he held steady. She relaxed and he was grateful.

"I told you, Danny, I'm okay and I can take care of myself."

"That's not the point. Do you know what to look for with an infection? Do you have any first aid experience? Have you let Doc Anders look at it?" he asked and caressed her hand with his thumb, stroking the top of it. She pulled her bottom lip between her teeth.

"I added new ointment and a new bandage. Won't that be enough?" she asked, sounding concerned.

Danny glanced at Mike. She looked from Danny to him.

"You should let me take a look at it. When does your shift today end?" he asked.

She hesitated a moment.

"Five, but I'm meeting someone," she added. Danny felt his gut clench. Was she involved with another man, or men? They would know. They'd had their eyes on her for a while. It had to be one of her girlfriends.

"When will you finish up with them?" Mike asked.

"I'm not sure. Listen, I'll be okay. I appreciate your concern. Don't feel guilty about the burn. It wasn't your fault. Now, would you like to order?" she asked.

Danny released her hand.

"Sure thing, honey," he said, and then they each gave their food order.

Marlena walked away.

"Who the hell is she meeting?" Danny asked.

"I don't know. Could be one of the women. Don't worry. She's not seeing anyone," Mike said.

"You go in at three today. See if you see her in town meeting up with some guy," Jack said then glanced back toward the kitchen. Danny felt disappointed and jealous. He didn't want to lose the chance at getting to know Marlena. They'd waited months to start flirting with her. They knew she was shy and they wanted to give her time to adjust to them. But she was real timid. So much so he started wondering about her past.

"Maybe we need to talk with Connolly," Danny suggested.

"What for?" Mike asked and took a sip of his ice tea.

"To find out what Marlena is hiding about her past. The more we talk to her, the more I get the feeling that she's scared. It's like she doesn't trust men. You saw her with the Dawn brothers, and she was just as shy and kept her distance from the table. That's not just from being timid. I think someone hurt her."

"Fuck, he's right," Jack whispered.

"Well, let's give it some more time. If she finds out we're snooping into her past, she'll never trust us," Mike said.

Danny exhaled as he watched Marlena go over to a table with one woman and three men. She seemed fine with them. Hell, she was even laughing. As he watched her hand over a bill to three women, she was just as friendly. Then she headed toward the Dawn brothers again and she looked on guard. Her shoulders straightened, she didn't come too close to the table, and she seemed on edge. There was something there and he wanted to know what. He liked her. Hell, he could see a whole future with Marlena and with him, Jack, and Mike taking care of her. What was she hiding? He really wanted to find out.

* * * *

Marlena finished her shift and headed out the back door of the diner. She needed to meet Parker by the hardware store in town. She got into her small beat-up Subaru that had seen better days and drove down the street to be closer. He was going to guide her in buying the right products for her to refinish the cabinets in the cottage.

Roy and Regan knew him well and had recommended talking to him about her plans so he could guide her. He came into the diner every week on Wednesdays and Fridays. They talked several times and then she finally asked him for his help. He was more than willing to help her. He was very nice and close to her age.

As she parked the Jeep she saw him standing there by his pickup truck waiting for her. He was a nice-looking guy and as she met him he leaned forward to kiss her cheek, shocking her. She wasn't attracted to him. She thought about Mike, Danny, and Jack and then wondered why. They weren't her boyfriends. They weren't even her friends although they seemed to be trying to get her to spend time with them.

"So, what do we need to do first?" she asked him and he smiled.

"You're so excited about this project. You have no idea how hard it's going to be. I think you'll be calling me for some help."

"No I won't. I told you I wanted to do this on my own. It's one of my many personal challenges," she told him as he held the door to the hardware store open and the owners greeted them.

She was trying to think about what she wanted the cabinets to look like and how intricate of details she could add, but Parker was right. This was harder than she thought. He helped her pick out the materials she would need as well as the stains, the topcoats, and some books. She'd already researched a lot at the library in town.

"I think you should take Parker's offer to help you get started, Marlena. You don't want to spend all this time and money and then have it come out all wrong," Mr. Phillips, who owned the hardware store, said.

She thought about it a moment and chewed her bottom lip. She didn't want to send the wrong messages to Parker. He was nice, but she hadn't expected him to greet her the way he had.

"I suppose so, but we should straighten a few things out first," she said as Parker's eyes lit up and he grabbed the first box of items to put into her car.

She waved good-bye and said thank you to Mr. Phillips as she carried out another box and Parker held the door open for her with his hip as he carried the heavier one.

They got to her car and she opened the trunk as they placed things inside.

"So, I can follow you home now, and we could figure out where to start and where to place the doors and things we need to refinish and stain. That way we can get started tomorrow. You get off at five again, right?" he asked.

She felt her heart racing. She wanted to ensure that he knew she wasn't interested in him in anything other than as a friend but as she went to bring that subject up, she heard Mike's voice. She turned around and there he stood, Mike in his deputy uniform, looking pissed off and in complete command. Her pussy actually spasmed with desire. Her heart raced and she knew she was done for. She liked Mike. Hell, she lusted for him and his brothers but she couldn't risk it all. She just couldn't.

"Good afternoon, Deputy Spencer. How are you?" Parker asked as he reached his hand out to shake Mike's. Mike shook his hand and then looked at Marlena.

"Looks like someone is planning on doing a project. What's with all that stuff?" he asked.

"I'm going to help Marlena refinish her cabinets in her kitchen. It's kind of tricky if you never did it before and she needs some guidance," Parker said but held her gaze, looking her over and smiling softly. She knew he liked her. This was so bad.

"Well, not the whole project, just to get started," she added, and Parker had a look of disappointment flash across his face and then it disappeared.

"We'll see. Refinishing work is hard. You work a lot of hours. It will be my pleasure to help you," he said.

Mike stepped closer to her.

He reached out and caressed a strand of her hair from her cheek.

"You should take it easy until those blisters heal. I want to get a look at them, maybe come over now and apply some ointment before rebandaging it," he said then gently brushed his thumb along her chin.

She glanced at Parker, who looked angry and insulted.

"I told you I'll be fine and can take care of it myself."

"I know you did, baby, but Danny, Jack, and I want to make sure our girl is well taken care of."

"Your girl?" Parker asked.

She looked at him and Mike nodded his head. "Yes, our girl."

"You staking a claim? The three of you for real? No bullshit?" Parker asked.

"Do I look like I'm bullshittin', son?" Mike said and Parker shook his head.

"I'll see you around, Marlena," Parker said, sounding upset, and turned around and walked away.

"Why did you do that? What did you mean saying those things to him?" she asked.

He stepped closer and placed his hands on her hips. "Settle down, honey. I did what needed to be done. No other men are going to come around and try to snag your attention. Not with my brothers and I around. We waited months to talk with you, to let you know how we felt. We understand that you're shy, that maybe you had some bad experience with a man before." Her eyes widened and she stepped back only to hit the back of the trunk. Mike pulled her closer. "Easy,

Marlena. Don't be scared, sugar. You feel the attraction just like we do. We'll take things slow. We'll let you get to know us. Let you ask us anything you want. We're planning on making you our woman. We're spreading the word."

She shook her head.

"But I don't want to be claimed. I don't want to be your woman. I want to be left alone. I can't accept this."

"Why not, sweetie? Did someone hurt you? Is that why you can't let down this guard you have up and see how sincere me, Danny, and Jack are?"

"Please, Mike, it's not fair, the way you're doing this to me."

He pressed closer and cupped her cheeks.

"Baby, tell me right now that you don't feel a thing for me and my brothers. Tell me, and I'll call it off. I'll accept it even though it breaks my heart and kills me inside. Tell me you don't feel a thing."

She stared into those gorgeous blue eyes of his. She felt the tears fill her eyes and her heart hammer in her chest. She never could tell a lie. She definitely couldn't tell one to Mike and in the damn deputy uniform, no less.

"I can't take the chance. I don't want to get hurt."

"We won't hurt you. Let us in, Marlena. Let us get to know you and what you're so afraid of."

She shook her head.

"Can't you let your guard down enough to get to know us so we can prove we're not bad men, and that we won't hurt you?"

She felt sick, angry that Peter had hurt her emotionally and physically so badly she lacked self-confidence and let him still beat her down even from miles and miles away.

"I'm scared to."

As she said the words and admitted them she felt like crying.

"Aww, baby, someone messed with you real good. But we're not him. You'll see that. Starting right now." He pressed his lips gently to hers, shocking her. But she didn't pull back. She absorbed the scent of his cologne, the feel of his masculinity surrounding her, and she let go. That kiss grew deeper and she wanted. She wanted, craved, lusted for more of him, and then she thought of Danny and Jack and she felt the same emotions for them. She was in trouble now. She'd let Mike kiss her. There was no turning back. She might have just made the next big mistake of her life.

* * * *

Mike released Marlena's lips despite the fact that he wanted more. He'd never felt so good kissing a woman. She was special. He ran his hand along her hip and stepped back.

"Thank you, darling. You pack a hell of a punch," he teased, and she pulled her bottom lip between her teeth and lowered her head.

She looked adorable, hell, edible, and his cock was hard as a steel rod against his pants.

He cleared his throat.

"Now about this project you're going to start. No need to worry, my brothers and I know a lot about these things. We can help you."

She started to shake her head and he raised one of his eyebrows up at her. "Now, now, don't be giving into those fears of us hurting you. That isn't going to happen. We'll take things slow and each get to know you, and you can get to know us. I can follow you back to your place now to get these things unloaded but then I need to get back to work."

"That's okay. I can leave them in the car or get them out myself. Don't leave work. The sheriff may get mad."

He smiled. "Not if I tell him I was helping you," he said and winked. She blushed and then shook her head.

"I must be losing my mind," she replied aloud without thinking and then headed around to the driver side of her car. Mike gave a wave and then headed to the patrol car. On the way to her place, he called Jack. Danny would stay at the bar and Jack would come help

Marlena set things up and unpack. They'd make plans for helping her with the cabinets and they would all get to know her better and make her feel safe. Maybe, they'd even get to learn about her past and the person who caused her to be so fearful? He wanted to know so he could make sure that person never came near their woman again. Never.

* * * *

Marlena had just finished putting the boxes onto the back porch when she heard the second male voice behind her. It was Jack's.

"So what's this about a new home improvement project?" Jack asked, walking onto the porch. She swallowed hard. Having one of them here was quite nerve-wracking. Having two made her shake a little. She hoped that Danny didn't show up, too. She just wasn't ready to be alone with the three of them.

"You didn't have to come over to help me, Jack. I'm capable of figuring things out on my own really," she added.

He approached, pulling her gently into his arms as if he had every right to do so. He cupped her cheek.

"Honey, you work so hard, so many hours on your feet, we would love to help you with this."

She was afraid he might kiss her. Had Mike told him that she let Mike kiss her in town? Did he think he had the automatic right to do that, too? Did she want him to?

"Whoa, hey, sweetie, what's wrong?" he asked, brushing his thumb along her lower lip as he bent slightly to look her in the eyes. *God, he's beautiful. Everything about him is beautiful.*

She looked down and away, causing his thumb to move from her skin. She felt the loss of his simple touch.

"Please don't touch me like that," she said.

"But I like touching you. I dream about touching you, kissing you, and feeling you next to me."

She shook her head. Was he serious? Did he really dream about her? God, these were the types of men she longed for, hoped for, tried to pretend that Peter was. And look where it got her. Maybe they were pretending, too?

"Don't do that. Don't say things to me that you think I want to hear or that other women like hearing. Don't," she said and pulled from his arms and walked over toward the door.

"I think you both should leave."

Mike looked at her strangely, like he was going to say something then held back. Was he thinking about telling her a lie? Maybe saying something she would want to hear to ease her uncertainty. Did she want him to? Did she want them to prove they were noble men?

"I'm heading back to work. I'll see you tomorrow. Let Jack help you. He knows a lot about these things," Mike said and tipped his hat toward her good-bye. She watched him go. The sexy way he walked in that uniform. He was the picture of authority, of protection and peace. The police back in Connecticut were nice, but they still told her she should disappear. Like the criminals had more rights than the victims. Peter would get away with attempted murder and arson. He would continue to get away with God knew what else.

She felt the masculine hand against her hip.

"Sweetie, what are you thinking about?"

She turned toward him, shocked that she was so lost in thought she had forgotten he was here still.

"Oh, nothing. Just tired," she said.

"Let's go inside and check out that kitchen of yours. Maybe tell me your ideas and your game plan," he suggested, and she nodded, allowing him to continue to hold her hand as they walked into the kitchen. She had flashbacks of the way she wished things could be. Her in the kitchen with Danny, Jack, and Mike helping her. Them laughing, enjoying one another's company, and then stealing kisses in between. They would eat together, laugh together, and make memories together. But when would it fall apart? When would they hurt her, cheat on her, hit her, try to kill her?

"Marlena," Jack questioned her as he held her shoulders and stared down into her eyes.

"Talk to me. Why are you scared? What are you thinking about when you get that lost look in your eyes?"

"Why are you here, Jack? Why do you and your brothers want to get to know me so badly? What do you want from me? Ultimately I'm not like Vicky?" she asked and he looked shocked.

He reached up and caressed her cheek. "We want to get to know you. Vicky is a liar. We never did anything with her even though she spread rumors. We like you, and the three of us rarely like the same woman. When we look at you we want more things."

"Like what?"

"Like a commitment, a partnership, a connection that lasts forever."

"How can you want those things with me when you hardly know me?"

"Haven't you ever heard of falling for someone and just knowing in your heart that they're right for you?"

She shook her head.

"That's not real life. That's in books and in movies. In real life things go wrong. People have their selfish reasons and desires for wanting to be with someone."

"That's not true, Marlena. Hell, take it from me, I'm a lot older than you. That may scare you, but in actuality it should bring you some peace of mind. I've dated a lot, hell I'm ashamed to say I did a lot of stupid shit, but that was years ago, that was before almost losing Mike."

"What?" she asked him. She could see the sincerity in Jack's eyes, the sadness at remembering. Could he be for real?

"Yeah, he was in the Navy. He was a Navy SEAL. He disappeared on a mission and was due home for our parents' anniversary party. He had the time scheduled off so when we hadn't heard from him, we knew something was terribly wrong. Anyway, weeks went by, then two months. He had fought his way out of enemy lines and a bad situation. One he has never spoken about and I'm certain never will. He came back a different man. He had a new outlook on life and he wanted to help others but also remain in a position of power and a soldier. He's taught Danny and me a lot and he's the youngest," Jack said and chuckled.

He stepped away from her and ran his fingers through his hair. He seemed nervous about revealing something personal to her. She reacted without thinking, letting her guard down.

"You're lucky to have a family, to have brothers who love you and who you love and care for."

"I know I am. I thank God every day. But what about you? No family at all?" he asked.

She shook her head and walked toward the refrigerator. She opened it and pulled out a water bottle, nodding toward him, silently indicating if he wanted one, too. Jack nodded back.

She closed the door and placed the water bottle onto the counter in front of him.

"I don't have any family. My mom died when I was finishing up college."

"Oh man, I'm so sorry, Marlena. That must have been terrible."

"It was hard, but she wasn't exactly mother of the year. She had problems. Luckily I had been working since I was fourteen and grabbing any extra hours I could to save money for college. I got a scholarship to Pace University in Westchester, New York. I never went back home. I got my degree and found a great job in Connecticut."

"Is that where you're from, Connecticut?" he asked, and she nodded her head and took a sip of her water. Jack did the same.

"Danny and I attended Universities in South Carolina. We hooked up with some guys running this cool business program and we loved it. Had money saved, took a chance on opening up a small bar in South Carolina near the colleges. We were in it with three other guys."

"Wow, that's impressive. What happened? Did it not work out?"

"It worked out great. We still have a financial share in the place but we're more like silent partners. It's a booming bar and club that expanded a few years back."

"Why didn't you stay there and run it full-time or open another place there if you were so successful?"

He looked at her and seemed a bit reluctant to tell her.

"What?"

"Mike was living here. We missed seeing our parents and being in Chance. When the property came up for sale where Spencer's is now, we grabbed it."

"Are you happy that you did? I mean you like it here? You want to spend the rest of your lives here?" she asked.

"I would say so. We've built our dream home way out a good fifteen miles from town. We enjoy helping out with the community and making sure it remains a great town where people are safe and inspired to settle down here. It's been expanding for years. Another set of storefronts are going in on the edge of town. Looks to be all locally owned and operated."

"I heard about those storefronts. We've been trying to convince Alicia to open up some sort of business of her own."

"That would be great. I know the guys in charge of the project. They even front the money for the right people with the right ideas."

"That's interesting. We'll see. She's a little hesitant to take the chance. Kind of shy."

"Like someone else I know," he said and reached out to press a strand of hair from her face.

She couldn't help but to smile at him.

He held her gaze and she held his.

"I'm really glad you didn't throw me out of your house," he said, and she laughed.

"What?"

"Back out there on the porch you seemed like you were giving Mike and me the boot. He had to leave, but I just got here."

"I let you inside, didn't I?" she asked, lowering her eyes.

"You offered me a drink, that's being friendly," he teased back.

She looked at him and he reached out and pressed a hand to her waist.

"We're not bad men, Marlena. I know we're older, but that just means we know what we want. We're not playing any games."

"I asked you what you wanted."

"And I gave you a rational answer about commitment, protection, and care. But what my brothers really want is you. All of you." He pulled her closer, reached up, and cupped her cheek.

"Now, darling, I'm going to kiss you, because I want to, and because I think you want me to, too."

His lips lowered and she debated about turning away and denying this attraction to him, but she couldn't, and when his lips touched hers she got lost in it, just like she got lost in Mike's kiss.

* * * *

Jack was consumed by this petite woman he held in his arms. She tasted so good, and felt even better flush up against his body. He ran his hand along her hip to her ass and squeezed her closer. She pulled back and their lips parted. She was gasping for breath.

"Oh God. Oh," she said and covered her mouth with her hand. He held her by her hips.

"You are one hell of a kisser, darling. I've been dreaming about those lips for months," he said, and she uncovered her mouth and shook her head.

"You don't believe me?" he asked and she shook her head again.

"Well you are. I could kiss you for hours. Hell, I could do a lot more than that. You smell edible, and not just like my mama's cooking either."

She seemed embarrassed as she gasped and stepped away. She sniffed at the sleeve of her blouse. "Oh God, I must reek of diner food."

He chuckled. "Like I said, you smell edible."

"Great. You also said like your mama's food."

"Our mama's a good cook. That's a compliment."

"Not after you kiss me and tell me my lips are addicting, that I'm edible, like your mama's food," she said, and he laughed aloud. She looked shocked and then she started laughing, too.

"I guess that might come across kind of creepy."

"Creepy? You're not kidding," she said and moved around the counter.

"Okay, so, back to business. Now that we got past the whole denial thing, let's talk about this kitchen and your ideas."

"The denial thing?" she asked.

"Sure, darling. You're denying you're attracted to my brothers and me. Now we know the feelings are mutual and we can move on from here."

"Really?" she asked with her hands on her hips, looking so damn sexy he felt his mouth watering.

"Really," he countered.

She walked around closer.

"Well, what if I told you that you made quite the assumption. Perhaps I was caught off guard by both you and Mike's charms."

"Our charms? Like what?"

"Like his uniform, a symbol of authority and power, and that thing he does with the one eyebrow raised up and his lip curls slightly. It's intimidating," she said, imitating Mike.

He chuckled. "You do a Mike impression pretty good."

She blushed and lowered her eyes.

"And me?"

"You're older, more experienced, and have a way with words. It gets me all confused and I don't know how to react."

He pulled her closer by her hands and placed them up on his shoulders as he sat at the barstool by the counter.

"It's called shock and awe, baby. Just you wait until Danny gets you alone."

Her mouth dropped open and she stuttered.

"Danny? I don't even know how I feel about kissing Mike and then you in the same day."

"You'll get used to all three of us kissing you, sometimes at the same time, with our lips exploring every inch of you."

She gasped and he pulled her closer and kissed her until she was limp in his arms. When he finally had his fill and felt that he got his message across, he dipped her slightly and stared down into her gorgeous green eyes as she held onto his shoulders.

"You're going to be our woman. You're going to learn to trust us as we learn to trust you. Now don't be scared. Follow your heart. I dare you to."

Chapter 5

Marlena couldn't help the exciting feeling she had inside all day long. She was going to start the kitchen project, but really she was excited and nervous about seeing the guys. She didn't know who would be coming over to help her today.

As she stopped by the counter where Adele was having a late lunch, she asked her another question about the Spencer men, and then Marlena asked her something too.

"So you think you can trust them? I mean to be alone with them in your house?" she asked.

Marlena worried her bottom lip and glanced around at the last few tables of the day.

"I think I can. I don't know. I'm just hoping they take things slowly and that I'll have the chance to run if I need to. I didn't expect them to be so persuasive. I really enjoyed talking with Jack yesterday. He was easy to talk to."

"And what about Mike? He can be intimidating with that serious expression he always has. He was in the military. You have to remember that men like that are resourceful."

Marlena exhaled. "I know. I could hardly sleep last night."

"I could imagine. But they seem like good men. How do their parents feel about them liking you?" Adele asked.

"I don't know. They haven't said anything."

"How about Danny? Do you think he'll be there to help you today and try to kiss you like his brothers did?" Adele winked.

Marlena chuckled and placed her hand over her heart. "Oh God please, Adele, I still don't know what to think of this or even if I want to take this chance. I'm a nervous wreck."

She heard the bell chime and Adele smiled. Marlena headed back to the kitchen for another order. She looked at the slip then checked the plates.

"You okay, Marlena?" Rita asked her. "You seem a little frazzled today."

"I'm okay, ma'am. Thank you," she said.

"If my sons are putting any pressure on you, or making you feel uncomfortable, then you let me know," Rita said to her.

"Rita." Roy said her name and gave her a stern expression. Rita pulled her bottom lip between her teeth and smiled.

Marlena wasn't sure how to take the fact that Roy interrupted his wife and seemed to be reprimanding her.

"Marlena." Regan said her name as he approached.

She held his gaze, feeling a little nervous.

"Honey, my wife worries about you, and she worries about her sons. You're a good worker, a sweet young woman. We're happy that our sons are staking a claim. We just want you to know that we're here for you, too. Rita especially, if you have any questions regarding this type of relationship. You're fairly new to Chance, and things might seem a bit different here, but they work out just fine."

"I appreciate that, sir."

"Regan. How many times do we have to tell you to call us by our first names. We're working here together as a team. Got it?" he asked and smiled.

"Got it. Thank you. I'd better get this food out there."

"Sure thing."

Marlena felt a little less uptight and a lot more encouraged by Regan's words. Truth was she didn't know much about these ménage relationships. Just what Mercedes explained and what she heard around town. Maybe she would ask the men. That would give her a better understanding.

As she delivered the food to her last table of the day, Adele waved good-bye, wished her luck, and gave her a hug. Marlena cringed when she heard the bell above the door ring. She thought she was done for the day. But the expression on Adele's face surprised her. Adele smiled.

"Looks like you'll be finding out how good of a kisser brother number three is. Good luck." She turned around and headed out the door saying hello and good-bye to Danny. Marlena locked gazes with him.

"Hey, beautiful," he said and eyed her over.

She placed her hands on her hips. "Hello, Mr. Spencer, counter or table?" she asked.

He looked around the place and stepped closer. "Counter where I'll wait for you to finish up so we can head to your place."

She raised one of her eyebrows up at him.

He gave her hips a tap. "To start the kitchen project. Get that mind out of the gutter, girl. I've got standards," he said and headed toward the counter, leaving her blushing and feeling turned on by him. She was in a heap of trouble.

* * * *

Marlena excused herself to get changed in the bedroom while Danny got things started in the kitchen. When she came out he was unscrewing the cabinet doors from the hinges and organizing the pieces.

"Okay, so what do we do first?" she asked and he smiled. He was waiting for this since talking to his brothers last night. He approached, looking at her in her skinny blue jeans and a black T-shirt with the V-neck that accentuated her large breasts. She was so petite and smelled so good even at the diner where she smelled like food. He approached her, wrapped an arm around her waist, and held her close. "First we need to get one major detail out of the way."

"What's that?" she asked, holding on to his forearms.

"Our first of many kisses," he said and leaned down and swept his mouth over hers. He kissed her deeply and when she moved her arms around his shoulders and kissed him back, he rejoiced inside. She wanted him, too. She was interested in this relationship between the four of them.

As he slowly pulled back, her eyes were still closed and then they fluttered open.

"Wow," she whispered.

"Wow, yourself, beautiful. Your kisses are addicting," he said and then kissed her lips gently and pulled back. He gave her ass a tap. "Now, back to work. Let's start with taking off the doors and keeping the screws and hinges together so we don't lose them for later when we put these back on."

She nodded her head and went right into working along with him. He hadn't done anything like this with a woman ever in his life. Nor had he ever met a woman who didn't mind working with her hands or breaking a nail. Marlena was his kind of woman.

* * * *

The music was playing and she was chuckling at a joke that Danny had made. They were covered with dust from sanding down the cabinets and then wiping away the dust.

"This wasn't too bad at all. I think we'll be good to go with the first coat of stain tomorrow," he said.

"I think so."

His phone went off and he glanced at it. Marlena watched him as his muscles flexed in his forearms and then she saw the bit of dust on his cheek. He texted back, and when she stepped closer she gently wiped the smudge away from his face.

He smiled.

"Thanks. That was Mike. Him and Jack are bringing over some dinner for us. Jack is heading over to the bar after."

"Oh they don't need to do that." She watched him cover his belly with his hand.

"Sure they do. I'm starving," he teased, and she smiled. She placed the cloth down onto the table then walked over toward the living room. She sat on the floor so she wouldn't get any dust on the couches. She looked back at their work and Danny joined her on the floor.

As she stretched out she wondered if the stain she picked would look right and then the top-coat once they made the cabinets look distressed.

She stretched her sore muscles and then Danny was taking her hand.

"You sore, baby?" he asked and she locked gazes with his blue eyes. He had a shadow of a beard and looked so rugged and sexy. Her heart pounded inside of her chest.

"Come in front of me and I'll rub your shoulders. You can't be going to work all sore tomorrow. My parents will have my head," he said, and she chuckled.

"They would not. You're their son, and they adore you."

He chuckled.

"There were probably times they wanted to disown me."

She eased in front of him between his legs, and the moment he touched her shoulders she felt the shivers. She was so attracted to him this was insane. She needed to focus on something else.

"Like what did you do to think they'd want to disown you?" she asked.

"Well, let's see, I kind of had a little rap sheet at a young age."

She looked over her shoulder at him.

"You? No way," she teased.

But then she closed her eyes and moaned as he worked her sore muscles with his hands.

"I stole a car once. I got into a bar fight and was arrested. I drank too much and nearly got kicked out of school my first year of college."

"My goodness you were a little bad boy. I don't know if we should be hanging out," she teased and went to sit forward, but he pulled her back between his legs.

She laughed.

He continued to massage her and told her about college and about the dorm he lived in. Very easily he had been manipulated into hanging with the cool crowd and trying to slide by with his grades. But his actions resulted in him almost failing out where his parents would have to pay for the college instead of have the scholarship money.

He eased his hands a little lower as he massaged her shoulders and maneuvered out toward the front of her chest. His fingers got closer and closer to her breasts and she so badly wanted him to touch her there. She felt needy, achy, and like she wanted more from him.

She eased back against his chest and then felt his one hand smooth down and over her breast. He massaged it as he kissed her neck and suckled against her skin. She could feel her breast tingling, the nipple hardening, and then she felt the cream drip from her cunt.

She was aroused and he moved her onto the rug, pressed his body partially over hers, and kissed her.

Marlena let him maneuver between her thighs and cup her one breast while he delved his tongue in deeper. He explored her mouth then kissed her lips while he massaged her breast and rocked his hips over her.

Marlena never felt so wild and needy as she ran her fingers through his hair then lifted her thigh up and against his thigh.

They were making out fully on the rug when they both heard the floor creak.

Danny held her cheeks between his hands and didn't look to see who it was. It was like he knew.

"Looks like we're having dessert before dinner," Jack teased and sat down on the couch next to her head.

"Don't let us stop you. We'll wait our turn," Mike said, and then walked toward the kitchen. He started talking about the cabinets but she couldn't concentrate. Not with Danny kissing her again and then rolling her to her side so he could lift up her top and explore her breasts.

"Danny." She said his name and he stopped what he was doing. He held her gaze and then gave her another peck on the mouth.

"You taste too good," he said.

"Dinner is here. We should eat. I have to be up early for work," she said and she could see the disappointment on his face as well as on the others. She sat up with his help and then Mike reached for her hand and pulled her up and into his arms.

"Hey, gorgeous. Miss me?" he asked and she nodded her head without thinking first. He smiled and then he kissed her.

She felt his hand massage over her ass and give it a squeeze. When he released her lips, Jack was there to take his place. He pulled her into his arms and hugged her tight.

"You tired, baby?" he asked and she nodded her head.

"We'll eat, then get you cleaned up and ready for bed."

"I don't think so," she said and pulled back as Danny opened up the boxes of pizza and two bottles of beer.

She swallowed hard as she watched them eat and guzzle down a couple of bottles of beer. They were big men. How may did they have to drink before they felt buzzed? She tried not to think about Peter and how he got drunk. He always went after the hard stuff then would come after her and insult her no matter who was there.

She put down the pizza.

"What's wrong? You don't like pizza?" Mike asked.

"Do you guys like to drink a lot? I mean alcohol?" she asked and then wished she hadn't. She was embarrassed. What was she going to do, ask them if they ever got drunk and said hurtful things then hit a woman?

"Baby, what kind of question is that?" Jack asked then took another slug of beer.

She stepped away from the counter and threw her paper plate into the garbage.

"Honey, does this have something to do with your fears and maybe someone who hurt you?" Danny asked her.

She swallowed hard.

"I just don't like overdrinking, or being around people who overdrink," she said and started to walk toward the living room, but Mike grabbed her and pulled her in front of him. He pressed her back against the counter so she couldn't move.

"Was the person who hurt you drunk when they did it?" he asked.

"What?" Danny asked.

"Mike, please."

Mike shook his head. "In order for this relationship to work, we have to be honest with one another. Talk to us. Explain your fears. Who was this guy that hurt you?" Mike asked as he cupped her cheek then pressed the loose strand of hair away from her face.

She lowered her eyes. "I don't want to talk about it. I'm not ready to."

"But this guy hurt you? He was an alcoholic?" Danny asked.

She nodded her head.

Jack stood up and walked closer. He rubbed her back trying to soothe her.

"I won't drink around you ever if it reminds you of him."

He was serious and she felt the tears in her eyes. He would do that for her? *They can't be real.* When were the real men, the manipulative assholes going to show their ugly faces?

"You don't have to do that. I just wanted to be sure that drinking wasn't something you do a lot or that you get drunk a lot. I mean you guys own and operate a bar. I don't expect you to not drink. I wouldn't ask you to not drink because of my stupid fears."

"Hey, your fears aren't stupid. We would do that for you. We want you to feel safe and cared for," Mike told her and he cupped her cheeks, leaned forward, and kissed her.

She wrapped her arms around his shoulders and hugged him tight when he released her lips. He ran his hands along her lower back and then to her ass. He massaged it as he suckled against the skin on her neck.

She kissed his neck in return and then things got a little wild.

* * * *

Danny lifted up Marlena's shirt and began to massage her shoulders and her lower back. She eased back up and Mike caressed under her shirt and used his hands to lift her top and cup her breasts. Jack placed his fingers against her cheek, turned her to the right, and kissed her deeply. They were all touching her together and Danny felt so possessive and turned on. She had a sexy body, with a firm, round ass that filled her jeans to capacity, and large breasts that were too big to cup with one hand. And they all had big hands.

Danny wanted to explore her body. He wanted to bring her pleasure and make her feel completely comfortable with him and his brothers touching her. Jack was kissing her deeply and she was moaning softly against his mouth. When Mike unclipped her bra, she tightened up, but Jack wouldn't release her lips and Mike was fast to soothe her concerns.

"Just getting to know this sexy body of yours, Marlena. We'll only go as far as you want us to. Relax and just feel. Let us make you feel good," he said then lowered his mouth to her breast.

Behind her Danny watched his brother's mouth latch onto a pink nipple as he massaged her full breast. Danny kissed her shoulder as he watched his brother explore and bring Marlena pleasure. He maneuvered his own hands around her waist to clasp on her jeans and then carefully unclipped them and pressed down the zipper. He suckled against her neck as Jack explored her mouth. She began to rock her hips and he knew she was aroused. He wanted to make her come. Right here in this kitchen. Right where they bonded and talked and shared their first kiss.

He maneuvered his fingers down into her pants and under her panties. She felt so hot and smooth.

"Fuck, baby, you are really warm down here. Are you wet, too? Are you liking three men loving this body together?" he asked then felt for her clit, pressed downward, and stroked a finger up into her cunt.

She pulled from Jack's mouth and gasped.

"Oh God. Oh, Danny, please. We need to slow down. I shouldn't be feeling this way."

"Yes, you should. You deserve to be cared for, catered to, and loved," Jack told her and then reached for her cheeks and kissed her deeply again.

Danny pressed her pants down lower and past her knees. He maneuvered closer behind her and rocked his hips against the crack of her ass so she could feel how hard his erection was. He stroked his fingers deeper and faster then pulled them out.

Mike shoved the chair out from under him and lowered to his one knee. He was working on her breasts.

Jack pulled from her mouth.

"Hold on to Mike's shoulders," he told her, and she did as she panted and rocked her hips.

Danny couldn't see what Mike was doing. He focused on his own plan as he spread her thighs and pulled one of her legs from confinement as he stroked her cunt from behind. She moaned again.

"Oh God please. Please." She begged for more.

Jack caressed her hair from her face.

"Let go, Marlena. Let us have that sweet cream. Come for us. Orgasm for your three men."

She shook her head and Jack continued to push her.

"You can trust us to care for you and to catch you when you fall."

Danny thrust two fingers into her cunt faster and faster. She was dripping with cream and he wanted to taste her. It would be difficult in this position, but he could do it. He needed to get her wetter and send her over the edge.

She was panting and moaning and as he stroked she spread her legs wider.

He pulled out his fingers and stroked her anus.

"Oh God," she gasped. Jack leaned down and caressed her as cheeks.

"You have a perfect ass, Marlena. Perfect." He ran his hand along the cheeks and pinched her ass cheek. She jerked and more cream dripped from her pussy.

"I think she likes that, Jack," Danny said.

"Just wait until she takes a cock in her mouth, her pussy, and her ass at the same time. She'll love that," Jack said and then pressed his finger over her puckered hole and pushed against it.

She shook and Danny lowered to his knees, pulled his fingers from her pussy, and suckled her cunt with his mouth. She bent forward more and Mike held her so that Danny could get better access to her pussy.

"Give him your sweet cream, Marlena," Mike ordered her.

"Oh God, this is so naughty. So bad," she cried out and then shivered. Danny felt her pussy explode and he licked and suckled until her clit was swollen and then Mike was lifting her up into his arms.

Danny leaned back on his heels and smiled at Jack.

"Delicious," he said, and Jack headed toward the couch where Mike held Marlena on his lap.

* * * *

Mike caressed her hair from her cheeks and held her tight.

"Are you okay, Marlena?"

She nodded her head.

Jack knelt on the floor next to her and Mike.

He reached out and caressed her thigh.

"I want to taste you, too. Will you let me?" Jack asked her.

She pulled her bottom lip between her teeth and then looked at Mike. Mike cupped her cheek.

"We all want a taste of what's ours."

Her cheeks turned a nice shade of red and then she nodded.

Mike smiled at her then kissed her nose.

"I want to taste you, too," she said, and Jack felt his heart begin to pound inside of his chest. He couldn't talk. He could hope that she meant what she just said.

Mike held her gaze. "You don't have to if you're not ready."

"I want to," she said and then she turned in Mike's arms and straddled his waist. She kissed him deeply and then she lowered down his body until her knees were on the rug and she began to unzip his jeans.

Behind her Jack caressed her smooth, round ass.

"I love this ass. I love the little sounds you make when you're coming." He stroked his finger up into her cunt as he spread her thighs wider. She gasped but then Jack heard Mike moan. Jack peeked to the side and saw Mike's cock disappearing into Marlena's mouth. His own dick hardened.

"Fuck, that's hot Marlena. You're so giving," Danny told her as he caressed her hair.

"Damn, Marlena, that mouth. Oh God, baby, that feels so good. So fucking good," Mike said, holding her head and thrusting upward lightly.

Behind her Jack stroked a finger from her pussy then over her anus. Every time he swiped her anus, it contracted.

He leaned forward and licked along each ass cheek as he thrust his fingers into her cunt. He was stroking quickly, turned on by the sight of her cream, her sexy body, and how giving she was.

He licked along her crevice.

She moaned louder and pressed her ass back.

Jack pulled one finger from her ass and maneuvered it against her puckered hole. He slowly pushed into the tight rings and entered her. In and out he stroked both her anus and her pussy. She rocked her hips faster. Her head bobbed up and down faster on Mike's cock and Mike moaned his release.

Marlena followed and Jack pulled his fingers from her body, lifted her hips, and suckled her cream as it poured from her pussy.

"My turn," Danny said and Jack moved out of the way. Danny lifted her up into his arms. She straddled his waist and he kissed her.

Jack looked at Mike, who was smiling and moving off the couch.

Jack looked at the gauze on her hip and the scarring that hit along her hip bone and upper thigh. It was definitely a burn of some sort.

He watched as Danny laid her on the couch, spread her thighs wide, and then feasted on her cunt.

Marlena sat there holding his head, panting and wearing only her T-shirt, her bra still undone and her breasts bobbing and swaying. Then Danny placed her thighs over his shoulders and he suckled and fingered her cunt until Marlena was screaming Danny's name and holding him to her chest.

Danny leaned up and kissed her deeply then held her in his arms as she wrapped her legs around his midsection and caught her breath.

She was amazing. She was their woman, and he wanted to know who hurt her, who scared her so much and possibly caused those physical scars. Whoever they were, he and his brothers would make sure that person never got near her again. Never.

* * * *

Marlena was shocked when Jack appeared with a warm washcloth to wash her up. She reached for the cloth. "I can do that."

He shook his head and pulled it from her grasp. He held her gaze. "That's our job. To take care of you, and cater to your every need."

She swallowed hard and when he was done, he leaned down and kissed the top of her pussy. She shivered, pulling her bottom lip between her teeth as Mike scooped her up, and placed her onto his lap. Danny placed a blanket over her.

They joined her on the couch and she wanted to ask them more about this relationship and how they felt it could work. She loved every minute with them. She loved what they just shared. She'd never felt so many emotions and such a connection before. It was wild.

"Why do you want to share me? What is it the three of you are looking for in a ménage relationship?" she asked.

Mike looked at Jack and Danny.

"I think the three of us want a woman we can all relate to, connect with on most levels, and to share our lives knowing that woman, you, would always be cared for," Danny told her.

"I think in some ways we feel like everything we have to give is even more, and a deeper connection and strength than if just one of us loves a woman and makes her ours," Jack added.

"I think it's all of that, and the simple fact that my brothers and I are close. We grew up with parents who love us and support us and who engage in a ménage relationship and are very happy. I like knowing that when I'm at work, or have to leave for a training or something, that my brothers are with you, protecting you," Mike said.

"You'll never be alone, I mean unless you want some alone time. It's not like we'd become your shadow. It's more like your protectors, your guardians, the ones that ensure you live a happy, loving life, and that you'll want to love each of us as well."

She thought about what they said and she played with her fingernails.

"It sounds so nice, so perfect. But I don't know if I can do this. I'm scared for a whole lot of reasons."

"But when we're with you, are you scared?" Danny asked her.

"No."

"When we shared what we did, when each of us were touching you, arousing you, and making you come, were you scared?" Jack asked.

"Sort of," she replied.

Mike cupped her chin.

"What do you mean sort of?"

"I never felt anything like it before. I wanted to please the three of you, but I was also getting pleasure from the three of you. It wasn't one-sided. It was equal."

"Exactly. And that's the way this relationship works. We're equal. One doesn't love the other more, we love together," Danny said to her.

"God, it's so much to take in and accept. I want to be with each of you. I want to feel more of what you made me feel. It's wild."

"It's real, not fake or forced," Jack said to her. He took her hand, brought it to his lips, and kissed her knuckles.

"Can you see yourself being with us? Living with us? Making love to us and giving us all of you as we give all of ourselves in return?" Jack asked.

She knew immediately that she could. Hell, she would ask them to stay the night right now if they had already been dating a while. They could think she was easy or desperate. Hell, did she have to tell them about Peter and what he did to her and how he could come looking for her?

"Yes. I can."

"Good, because in a few minutes I want another taste of that sweet cream," Danny told her and ran his hand between her legs, and she wiggled from his touch and maneuvered off of Mike.

She stood up, wrapped the blanket around her waist, and held their gazes.

"I don't think that's a good idea," she said.

"Why the hell not?" Jack asked, standing up in front of her.

She held his gaze. "Because then I'll ask you to stay the night, and make love to me."

They all stood up. Danny pulled her closer and cupped her cheek.

"And what would be so bad about that?" he asked.

"We haven't even gone out on a date yet. What would you think of me, jumping into bed with three men who haven't even asked me on a real date?" she teased, feeling her cheeks warm.

"The woman's right. We're going about this ass backwards," Danny said, taking her hands into his.

Jack moved in behind her and grabbed her hips and rocked his cock against her ass. "With an ass as perfect as hers, ass backwards is fine with me." He kissed and suckled her neck, making her giggle then smack at his shoulder.

"Let's make it official. Dinner tomorrow night?"

"But we have to finish this kitchen," she said.

"Well, I'm fine with dinner here tonight being our first date, if you are," Danny said, teasing her.

God was she tempted, but she wanted to do this right.

"No can do. A real date, so I don't feel so easy," she said.

"Not easy. We've been hinting at liking you, wanting you for over six months. Definitely not easy," Mike told her.

"So the lunches and breakfasts don't count either?" Danny asked as he pushed the blanket down and off of her, wrapped his arm around her waist, and cupped her bare pussy.

"Danny!" she scolded, and Jack and Mike chuckled.

"Dessert again it is," Mike said, and Danny carried her to the couch, lifted her so her back was against his front, and spread her thighs over his open thighs. She faced Mike and Jack.

"Brothers, look what I got for you," he said and he cupped her breasts, and Mike fell to his knees and stroked her pussy.

"Get ready, baby, we're going to break you down and get you used to this triple action," Mike said then began to feast on her pussy. His brothers cheered.

"Oh yeah, triple action strikes again," Jack said and Marlena moaned her first release and wondered if she would have the willpower or the strength to make them go home tonight when really all she wanted was for them to stay.

Chapter 6

"Okay spill the beans now, woman," Mercedes said as Marlena stood by the table with Adele and Alicia. She'd called for this meeting and Mercedes knew that her project with Danny and his brothers had progressed further and faster.

As she explained what went down, they were smiling wide.

"Oh God this is great. They're perfect for you. Why the hell didn't you just sleep with them last night?" Mercedes asked.

"Duh! You know why," Marlena said and looked around the diner. It was slow now. The rush would be in soon.

Adele touched Marlena's hand. "Honey, you like them a lot. They obviously care about you and the chemistry is there. You should take the chance and see where this goes."

"And if they turn out to be using me, then what? Besides, I don't think I can let it go that far. Not yet, anyway," Marlena said, lowering her eyes and worrying her bottom lip.

"Marlena, I'm the last one to give advice to anyone about men. I lost more than I can explain because of my poor decisions. But, time heals everything. Moving here to Chance, the four of us finding one another was fate. We support you no matter what decision you make. But know this, don't let that man from your past dictate your future. There's differences between him and the Spencer men. You know it. You feel it," Alicia told her.

"I know that. I do. In my head, at least."

"No, in your heart and in your body, from what you described took place in your little cottage last night," Mercedes teased. They all chuckled and Marlena's cheeks reddened. She looked around the diner and made sure no one was listening. They were in the corner away from anyone and whispering low.

"I'm scared. For more reasons than I shared with the three of you."

Mercedes looked at the others. What had Marlena left out about the man from Connecticut who was alcoholic and abusive?

"What I didn't tell you is that Peter, well, he could be looking for me."

"What?" Adele and Alicia asked at the same time. Mercedes took Marlena's hand.

"Honey, shit, why didn't you tell us?"

Marlena wiped the tear from her eye before it escaped.

"I'm embarrassed by it. I don't want to face the fact that I could have to hightail it out here one day with no notice, no explanation, and just disappear."

"No, honey. No, you can't live your life like this. What did he do to you? I mean like being verbally and physically abusive is one thing, but what else that he could come after you?" Adele asked her this time.

Marlena took a deep breath and looked around the diner. She turned sideways and showed them her burn scar from Peter that sat below the raw, red skin from the coffee burn.

"This burn. The one I said happened when I was younger, well, it happened less than a year ago, and right before I came here and found Chance."

"How?" Alicia whispered with tears in her eyes.

Marlena looked so scared. Mercedes could see her shaking.

"Well," she started to say and closed her lips tight then forced the words from her lips as tears fell. "He tried to kill me, by setting fire to my apartment and the building with me in it."

"Oh Jesus," Mercedes said and stood up and pulled Marlena into her arms.

Marlena immediately pulled back.

"No. Don't let anyone see us like this. They'll ask questions. They'll be concerned. It's that type of town. It's perfect here," she said and wiped the tears from her eyes, took a deep breath, and straightened out her shoulders.

"I don't think I can be intimate with Mike, Danny, and Jack. I don't know if I can let the walls down and take that chance. There are three of them. Mike was a Navy SEAL. Do you know what damage he could do to me alone?"

Mercedes shook her head. "No, no, sweetie, they're not like that Peter guy. When they look at you, and watch you, they have love, respect, and compassion in their eyes. You can see it."

Marlena shook her head.

"You're just saying that."

"No she isn't. We've all seen it. Hell, I wish someone would look at me like that," Alicia added.

"It's special, Marlena. You need to be honest with them. Maybe tell them about Peter, even if it's just so that they're aware and can protect you," Adele said.

Marlena shook her head.

"I can't tell them about Peter and what he did. I can't let them know how stupid I was, how gullible and overtaken by Peter and his dominant personality. They could use it to control me. They could think I'm weak. I can't let my defenses down no matter how good it makes my body feel."

"Marlena, it's more than sexual, more than physical, and you know it. We've seen you looking at them and watching their every move and shaking like a leaf when they come too close. You obviously felt pretty damn comfortable with them last night to let them get as close to you as you did," Mercedes said to her and raised one of her eyebrows at her in challenge.

"Yeah, well, I was unprepared for the triple attack. They can be pretty commanding and sexy when all three of them are in action," she said, her cheeks reddening again. The girls laughed.

"That good, huh?" Adele asked and wiggled her eyebrows up and down in a silly way. Marlena laughed. Then she looked very serious again as she whispered to them.

"I won't place them in danger. I won't bring them into my mess from my past that will eventually rear its ugly head. They'll hate me."

Mercedes shook her head.

"No, honey, they won't hate you, but they'll be angry if you don't tell them, if you don't give them the chance to help you and instead one day you disappear. Then they'll hate you, and Peter would have won no matter what the outcome."

Marlena stared at her, tears filled her eyes, and the door to the diner chimed, indicating another customer had arrived. It was Sheriff Gordon.

She straightened her shoulders. "Well, back to work."

They watched Marlena greet the Sheriff, who immediately looked at Alicia and tipped his hat at all of them. "Good afternoon, ladies," he said. They all smiled and said hello.

"Alicia," he said to her.

Mercedes had to hide her smile. It seemed the Sheriff had a thing for Alicia, but Alicia, too, was too shy, and too unwilling to trust a man. Hell, this was why they all got along so well. They were all burned by men. Their hearts ripped out and stomped on. It would take an army to get each of them to open up their hearts. Well, for Mercedes it could be three. But who was she kidding. The Dawn men weren't her types at all.

The sheriff went to sit down by the counter and Marlena was her smiling, friendly self. But Mercedes worried about her.

"I'm worried. Marlena never mentioned that her ex could be looking for her, or that he tried to kill her and that's how she sustained the burns on her hip bone," Alicia said to her and Adele.

"I know. I was thinking the same thing. Hell, we all haven't poured our guts out about what happened in our pasts to make us this hard and timid of men. But we explained enough that we can empathize and understand. Marlena likes Mike, Danny, and Jack. Her eyes light up when she talks about them, and whenever one of them is around. They could protect her. Mike is a deputy and this town is tight-knit," Adele said.

"You're not kidding. I swear, sometimes when I get into town and I'm walking around, it's like men have their eyes on me, like they're guarding me. Some guy was passing through town the other day and stopped to ask me directions, and before I could respond, Monroe Gordon appeared out of nowhere and spoke to the guy. Then when the guy drove off, Monroe gave me the third degree about getting too close to a vehicle I didn't know, and how I could have been taken. It was like the third degree on safety."

Mercedes and Adele chuckled.

"Honey, by the way the sheriff looks at you, and how his brother Monroe did that, I'm surprised you haven't figured out that they like you and want to protect you," Mercedes told her. Alicia looked stunned and downright shocked.

"Has Caldwell Gordon shown up out of the blue, too?" Adele asked her.

Alicia nibbled her bottom lip.

"Oh my God, I was looking at the number to call on the sign about the new storefronts going in on the edge of town. There's a small one on the corner unit, and I was thinking that maybe I could start a business there. You know, maybe a consignment store where I can sell my stained-glass art, and others who make jewelry and things. Plus there's Mia, who makes those gorgeous hats, Louise, who makes her scarves, and a bunch of others that I've met here in town. With more people passing through Chance, it could be great to advertise it as locally made items."

"That would be awesome. Your stained-glass pieces are gorgeous, Alicia. You could do it," Adele said, and Mercedes nodded her head in agreement. She knew that Alicia had wonderful ideas, but to actually have the nerve to take the chance and do it was completely different.

"Anyway, Caldwell pulled up along side my car in that sports car he has."

"It's a Porsche, Alicia. An expensive one," Adele said.

"Well, he asked me if I was okay and what I was doing. I told him and he told me it was a great idea and that if I needed financial backing that he would be there. Or if I had questions on running a business since him and Monroe have numerous ones. It was so weird. I wondered why he would offer financial backing to a complete stranger," Alicia said to them.

"You're not a complete stranger. They've talked to you in town at some of the local events, and they seem to pop up to protect you or just watch over you when you least expect anyone to be around."

"They're too intimidating. Too wealthy and kind of demanding. You've seen the way the sheriff is," Alicia whispered and looked toward him. He was talking to Marlena as Marlena placed his food onto the counter.

"He's gorgeous and pretty damn sexy in that high position of authority. Is that what scares you about him, and his brothers?" Mercedes asked. She knew that Alicia's ex was similar. He had been controlling and used her savings to invest in some business she wanted to do and it failed.

"Yes, all of the above. I don't need that type of man in my life. Been there, done that."

"Alicia, you're attracted to that type. We all are. But it doesn't mean they'll be like your ex."

"Adele, I hear you. I process it in my head, but my heart aches and my stomach feels queasy at the thought of trusting another man again, never mind more than one. No thank you. I'll just try to focus on this store and whether I have the nerve to risk what I have saved. It took a year to make back some of the money I lost. I think we should worry about Marlena. She's the one we need to protect and help guide through this. She needs to tell Mike about her ex and the possibility that he could come looking for her."

"Let's give her some time to accept them. I have a feeling their relationship is going to be going to the next level pretty damn quickly," Adele said as the door chimed and Mike came in with Deputy Taylor to have lunch.

Mercedes felt her belly tighten and she quickly looked away.

"Looks like we're not the only ones who are interested in some men in Chance," Adele teased, and Alicia chuckled.

"Ladies, good afternoon," Taylor said as they looked up and he tipped his hat at them. Mike said hello then headed straight toward the counter where Marlena was still talking to the sheriff. *Looks like living in Chance is about to get even more interesting.*

* * * *

"Good afternoon, Marlena," Mike said as he greeted Marlena hello. He placed his hand on her hip as he removed his hat and held it in his hand. She touched his forearm and seemed hesitant.

"Good afternoon, Deputy Spencer, Deputy Dawn. Do you need a table or is the counter okay?" she asked them.

"Counter is good," Taylor said and smirked. Mike felt a bit upset that she didn't want to respond to him after last night at her place.

He caressed her arm then reached up and cupped her cheek. Holding her gaze, he lowered his mouth to hers.

"Is that any way to greet one of your men?" He didn't give her a moment to answer. Instead he kissed her softly on the lips then released them and gave her hip a tap.

"That's a lot better, beautiful."

She pressed her lips together and then glanced at the sheriff and Taylor before looking back at him. Placing her hand on her hip, she gave him a hard look.

"Feel better now?" she asked.

The sheriff and Taylor chuckled.

Mike smiled as he sat down by the counter next to the sheriff. "It will do for now, sugar. How's your day been so far?" he asked her.

"Busy. Can I get you an ice tea or coffee?" she asked.

"Ice tea," he replied and then headed behind the counter. He stared at her ass in the tight black skirt she wore. The woman was built to more than satisfy him and his brothers. She was sexy as damn hell. But what pissed him off was that he wasn't the only man watching her. He glared to the right to see two men he didn't recognize, sitting at the other end of the counter. Marlena put down the glasses of ice teas for Mike, Taylor, and the sheriff, then headed down that way. She reached for the pot of coffee, and as she bent to pick up the napkin that fell, both men peered over the edge of the counter, either trying to get a better look at her breasts or her ass.

He was about to get up when the sheriff spoke.

"So, rumors are true? You and your brothers staking a claim to little Miss Marlena?" he asked.

"It's true," Mike said but kept an eye on the guys and on Marlena. She headed back toward them.

"You need to make it official. Did I miss your call for a meeting in my office?" the sheriff asked.

Mike shook his head. He knew the rules. Every woman was cared for and watched over in Chance. When men wanted to claim a woman and start courting her, making her officially theirs, then they needed to officially inform the sheriff. He sort of gave the okay, but it was more like protocol they followed. Too many times over the years, men came to live in town for a few months as if they were making a permanent residence and then they would say they were interested in the same woman and wanted to share. Turned out to be a game for them and women got hurt. Badly. This was a way to ensure there was no bullshit. Sometimes women came into town and did the same thing. Marlena had been living here for six months. The sheriff was being cautious.

"We'll make that appointment. We're still trying to figure Marlena out."

She returned to them and asked if Mike and Taylor were ready to order since the sheriff already had his lunch.

He gave his order, and Taylor gave his.

"Hey, Marlena, are you and your friends planning on attending the clam festival on the weekend? It's a fundraiser for the Godfrey boys and their family who lost their house in the fire two weeks ago."

"Oh my, is that this weekend? I didn't realize. Mercedes, Adele, Alicia, and I talked about attending. Alicia knows the mom and Mercedes became friends with the family. I'll ask them. They're right over there. Unless, Mike, you and your brothers don't think I've time, with us working on my kitchen," she said to him.

"You'll have time. We have all week, plus there's always Sunday that we could stain and finalize everything. It's coming along well," Mike said.

"Great. Let me talk to the girls and see if they still plan on attending. Are you and your brothers going to be there?" she asked Taylor. Mike felt his gut clench. He hoped she wasn't interested in them, too. Wait, she couldn't be. She was so shy and fearful last night, and she indicated she had gotten hurt before and wanted to be cautious. *God, I'm so jealous of everyone.*

"I think so. I need to check with them." Taylor said.

"How about you, Max? The brothers attending the event?" Taylor asked the sheriff.

"I think they will be. I'll just be stopping in for a bit," Max told them.

Mike watched her walk over to her friends' table.

"She's a gorgeous woman. You and your brothers lucked out big time. She's really sweet, too," Taylor told Mike, and Mike nodded his head and thanked him. They did get lucky, but there was still a lot to learn about her and her past.

* * * *

Marlena was relieved when Mike, Taylor, and the sheriff left the diner. It made her very nervous, and for some strange reason, she felt guilty. It was like she was the bad person and did something wrong in her past and that hiding it was being dishonest. It made her think about Peter and also about Detective Morgan. Could she call the detective and find out an update? Or should she just forget about Peter, Connecticut, and the past and move on? Last night after the men left her house, she had terrible nightmares. They were worse than the usual ones where she was caught in the flames in her apartment. In these, she actually got burned and felt the excruciating pain. She could have woken the dead, her screams were so loud. It woke her up as she gasped for breath. She was soaked, too, and needed to change her T-shirt.

Right now she felt a bit of an anxiety attack coming on. She stepped outside in the back of the diner a moment to catch her breath and ease her mind of the nightmares. She closed her eyes and let the warm, beautiful sun caress her skin. She loved it here. She really felt that Chance was the place she was meant to find and to live a new life. It made her want things. Things that hadn't crossed her mind since being hurt physically and emotionally by Peter.

She gasped and jumped to the side in a fighting stance as the door loudly opened.

Regan was standing there looking concerned.

She covered her chest with her hand and caught her breath.

"Shit. I didn't mean to scare you. Are you feeling okay? You seem distracted and then I heard you breathing kind of funny."

"I'm okay. I just needed a breath of fresh air and this beautiful sun that's shining today," she said and smiled then headed toward the door. Regan stopped her by touching her hand.

"Sweetie, you know that Rita, Roy, and I care about you? That you're more than just an employee here? And not because something is brewing between you and our three sons either." She felt the emotions get the better of her. She watched the way Roy, Rita, and Regan interacted with one another and around their sons, too. It made her long for things she never really had. For family, for parents who would love her and could help her deal with this problem she had. But they weren't hers to have. She was alone, aside from her three new best friends. That had to be enough.

"I appreciate that, Regan. You're great bosses and I love it here. I wouldn't want to leave, unless I really had to."

He scrunched his eyebrows together. "You planning on leaving?"

She pulled her bottom lips between her teeth.

"Honey, are you in some kind of trouble?" She began to shake her head in denial but Regan held his hand up for her to not even bother.

"This town is more special than I think you realize. There are people here that protect and watch over every one of us. The men are supposed to watch over the women so they feel safe, secure, and are able to live full, happy lives. It's how the town operates. So let's say that you're running from something, or someone from your past, from before coming to Chance. You can tell the sheriff and he'll be able to help you with everything. We all look out for one another. We've got rules that need to be followed. So please, if you need help. If you're confused, overwhelmed, or just need people who can help and will care for you, then talk to us. We're here for you," he said.

"Is everything okay?" Rita asked as she approached wiping her hands on her apron.

"You know Rita always wanted a daughter. You're sweet, you're beautiful, and remind me a lot of Rita. Don't think that you're alone. Okay?" he asked, and Marlena couldn't help herself. She hugged Regan tight and then pulled back, forcing the tears away.

"I'd better get back," she said, her voice filled with emotion as she exited the kitchen and came back to two tables and a new one. Four more hours and she could head home to work on the kitchen with one of the guys. Whom, she didn't know, but she didn't care. She felt safer with one of them around, and that in itself was enough to swallow and get used to.

As she took the orders and waited on the tables, she thought about the town, the rules, and Mike, Danny, and Jack. Could she trust them enough to tell them about Peter? Could it turn them off or make them push her away? Was it better to find out now before she fell deeper for them? She felt that anxious feeling deep in her belly. She needed to make a decision and soon. She didn't want them to hate her, but like her friends said, if they found out later, when she had to disappear, it would be worse, and maybe she would lose them forever.

* * * *

"What was that all about, Regan?" Rita asked her husband as she placed her hand on his arm. She could see the shocked expression on his face. When Marlena hugged him, there was sadness in her eyes and such emotion. She hightailed it outta there quick.

"I don't know," Regan said and looked toward Roy. His eyes filled with concern as he flipped the burgers and held their gazes.

"She's scared, isn't she? Is it from our boys? Are they pushing her, or asking too much too soon?" Rita asked. Regan knew that their sons were demanding men and were older than Marlena. He understood his wife's concern about them pushing Marlena too far too quickly. Especially with Marlena being new in town and unused to the ways a ménage relationship works. But there was more going on here with Marlena. If she were in some sort of trouble, he hoped Marlena would confide in his sons. They would protect her.

"I don't know. I don't think so. I think it's more. You know as well as I do we saw something in her eyes that day she came here looking for work," Reagan said to her.

She pulled back and clasped her hands in front of her.

"You thought she might have been in trouble," Rita said.

"I think she is still. I think she's holding back and maybe feels like she's got to protect herself from everyone and everything."

"The men will get it out of her. It's their job now if they're officially staking a claim," Roy said then pulled the burgers off the grill, placed them on the buns with the fries, and put them on the shelf. He tapped the bell.

"Although they haven't made it official. Maybe we need to talk to them, Reagan," Roy said and then turned back around as Marlena came in to grab the order. She looked as normal as anything. She smiled at them.

"Got two more tables. Are there more chicken specials left or not?" Marlena asked.

"Two more, honey," Rita told her and smiled.

"Great. I'll be right back after I confirm they want those." She turned around and headed out.

"She's so sweet, and petite. I hope she's not in trouble, or that she's on the run," Reagan said.

"On the run? What?" Rita asked.

"She said she loved it here and didn't want to leave. It was almost like she was setting me up to not be shocked if that happened."

"That doesn't sound right at all," Rita replied and didn't like the feeling she had now either.

"If she's in trouble, then we need to help her."

"And how are we supposed to do that?" Roy asked.

"You leave it to me. I'll get her to talk, to come around and see we can be her family if need be. I like her. Hell, she reminds me a lot of myself at twenty-three. We'll make her see she's cared for and there's no place better than Chance. You two talk to the men. Make sure they're taking their time, and you know what I mean," she said and raised one eye up at them.

They chuckled.

"You watch that sassiness, woman, or there'll be hell to pay tonight," Roy challenged.

"Bring it on, Roy, I can handle both of you, remember?" she teased and went back to preparing more food.

"Oh I recall someone begging for mercy just last night," Reagan teased her and gave her a slap to her ass. She gasped just as Marlena came into the kitchen.

"Oh, I'll just come back in a minute."

"Get back here. She's my woman. I can tap that ass if I want to."

"Reagan," Rita scolded and the men chuckled.

"They can be a handful. But believe me, I've got them wrapped around my finger. So do you need those two specials?" Rita asked Marlena.

"Yes, ma'am," she said and smiled softly.

"You got it," Rita said and went back to working. She caught Marlena smiling, and Rita hoped she could see the love between Rita and her men. Marlena could have that, too, if her sons gained her trust and helped her to see that they could love her and protect her no matter what. Maybe she should talk to the men, and not Roy and Reagan.

She smiled then went about cooking. She'd get to it later. Give the men a chance. They only made their first move last week. She smiled. Maybe in a few months she would gain herself a daughter-in-law and a grandbaby?

"What's that's grin about?" Regan asked her.

"Oh nothing. Nothing at all."

Chapter 7

Marlena laughed as Danny cursed for hitting his thumb again. She could see it bruising and swelling up as she climbed down from the small stepladder and walked toward him.

"Let me see," she said and chuckled. He really wasn't very good at this construction stuff. She reached for his hand.

"I'm fine. Shit," he carried on. She smiled.

"I'll get you some ice." She walked toward one of the boxes on the floor, opened it up, and pulled out a box of plastic bags. She took one then went to the freezer and grabbed some cubes. She sealed the bag then brought it over to him. He was sitting on one of the chairs by the kitchen and living room.

"Here. Place this on for a little while." She put her hands on her hips as she watched him put the bag of ice on.

"You really aren't too comfortable doing this type of work, are you?" she asked.

He went to speak then stopped. He started again.

"I'm not, but I was hoping to impress you anyway," he told her and winked.

She walked closer. She couldn't help but to touch him. He was so handsome and a bit different than Jack and Mike. Danny was not so intimidating as he was forward. He said what was on his mind and didn't seem to sugarcoat much. But he was hiding his dislike of doing work like this.

She pushed a strand of hair from his eye and held his gaze.

"Your brothers force you into this?" she asked and stepped back.

But he placed a hand on her waist and pulled her between his thighs.

"I wanted to be able to spend time with you and get to know you just like Jack and Mike do. It's not like I don't entirely know what I'm doing."

"Well, I would hope you knew enough. I think we're almost ready to stain the doors and the cabinets. I saw Parker Cass in the diner today. He said if we needed help, he would come over," she teased. Meanwhile Parker did come in and she found out that he had a thing for Alice. She was hoping they would get together, probably as badly as her friends hoped Marlena would get together with the Spencer brothers.

Danny pulled her closer and lifted her up so that she had to straddle his hips or fall on her ass. She gasped and grabbed on to his shoulders.

"You think that's funny? Poor guy could have gotten a bullet in his ass from Mike."

"What?" she asked, holding his gaze. He used his hands to rub up and down her bare thighs. She was wearing a pair of cotton shorts and a tank top. It was pretty warm in the house. He ran those hands up her hips then under her tank top and pulled her closer.

He held her gaze and she held his. Those damn blue eyes told so much about him. Danny was a businessman, and he had power, control, and a bit of arrogance about him. She felt her pussy clench. He turned her on and he knew it.

"Ever get a spanking for being naughty, Marlena?" he asked, shocking her. She shook her head and he used his thumbs to manipulate her nipples over the tank top as he held her under her arms. His hands were so big, and his fingers thick and long, that he could reach the tiny buds and stimulate them.

Her lips parted.

"You know, I think you deserve a little spanking, for bringing up Parker, and for teasing me about hitting my thumb again."

She shook her head, nibbled her bottom lip, and held his gaze. She couldn't believe how turned on she was at his naughty words.

"Is there anything I can do to make it up to you? I was just teasing."

He reached up and ran a thumb along her lips, staring at them. She didn't know what came over her, but she was aroused and felt like giving Danny a little bit of his own medicine. She peeked her tongue out and licked a small part of skin on his thumb.

He held her gaze and pinched her nipple with his other hand.

"I could think of some things that might save your sexy little ass from turning pink by my hand."

"Like what?" she asked, opening wider. He pushed more of his thumb between her lips and she sucked on it and pulled it between her lips.

He pulled harder on her nipple and she closed her eyes and rocked her hips on his lap. He pulled his thumb from her mouth and trailed it down her throat between her breasts then pushed the material aside and cupped her breasts. She gasped. Felt her pussy cream and she moaned.

"You are so responsive, baby. So fucking responsive." He pulled her breast from confinement and leaned down to lick her nipple.

She grabbed a hold of his shoulders and pressed upward so he could get a full mouthful of her nipple and breast.

She moaned aloud and then gasped when she felt the second set of hands on her shoulders from behind.

"Mike," she moaned.

"Damn, I've got good timing," he said then ran his fingers through her hair, tilted her head back, and kissed her. She reached up and held onto his cheeks and head as he ate at her mouth and Danny feasted on her breasts. She'd never felt so out of control. She never wanted to have sex so badly in her life, and that thought had her pulling from Mike's lips.

"We have to stop. Oh God, Danny, please." She begged for him to release her breast. He pulled on her nipple, twirled his tongue around the areola, then released it.

"I want you," Danny told her then cupped her face between his hands and kissed her deeply. She held onto him, even as she felt him stand up with her wrapped around his waist as if she weighed nothing at all. She felt them walking and she pulled back.

"Wait. Oh God, we can't. God," she said and banged her forehead against his chest.

They were in her bedroom. Danny sat down with her still straddling his waist. Mike caressed her hair from her cheeks.

"Talk to us. Explain what's going on."

She lifted her head from Danny's chest and held Mike's gaze.

"I can't take this chance. I'm sorry, but I can't."

"Because of him? Because of this asshole who hurt you?" Danny asked, sounding angry.

She nodded her head.

Mike crossed his arms in front of his chest.

He looked so big and powerful even out of uniform.

"Why don't you explain a little more about this guy? Make us understand what's holding you back?" Mike asked. She eased her way off of Danny's lap. She stared at both of them. She saw the bed, looked at their bodies in the jeans, the T-shirts, and those sexy, older expressions. It turned her on and made her want to throw inhibition to the wind.

"Let's go back out into the living room," she said and went to leave. Mike grabbed her hand.

"No. Let's talk right here. It's obvious that being in your bedroom alone with us makes you nervous. Why?" he pushed.

"Mike, please. Let's just go into the living room," she said, feeling that anxiousness begin to deepen. She was getting frazzled and freaked out.

He pulled her closer. He ran his hand along her hip and cupped her breast gently. She pulled back. He pulled her against him again.

"You're practically shaking. We would never hurt you," Mike told her.

"Did this guy you were with, did he hurt you, Marlena? Did he abuse you?" Danny asked and she felt the tears hit her eyes.

"Let's go back out," she said but didn't move. She felt like if she did move then even that would make her cry. Make the tears flow and she would break down and tell them everything.

"Why are you scared of being in this bedroom with us?" Mike pushed for answers. He was being a boss, a law man, running the show, and she got angry, and it put her on the defensive.

"It's better if we go into the kitchen and finish working," she said slowly.

"No. We want you in here. Why do you want to leave us?" Danny asked, standing up and taking her other hand. They both stepped closer, holding her hands and bringing them to their chests, palms flat.

"Why?" Mike pushed.

She lowered her head.

"Because I won't be able to stop. I'll want to keep feeling everything you make me feel and I shouldn't let it happen."

She felt Mike's fingers under her chin tilting her face up toward him.

"But it's right, what we feel. My brothers and I want you. We want to make you happy, protect you—"

She shook her head, cutting him off.

The tears filled her eyes.

"You can't protect me. I have to protect you."

"From who?"

She heard the third voice and turned to see Jack standing there. He was dressed nicely. He must have come from Spencer's.

"Please don't make me tell you. It's embarrassing and it will only make leaving worse."

"Leaving? You're leaving?" Jack asked, coming into the room, too, and standing next to Mike.

"Eventually I'll have to," she said.

"Why?" Jack asked.

She was silent a moment and Mike touched her chin.

"Why?" he asked firmly.

"Because he tried to kill me once, and he might be looking for me to finish the job." The tears spilled down her cheeks and she stood there staring at their shocked expressions, wondering if she just made a huge mistake, trusting them with this information.

"Marlena, you need to explain all of it to us, so we can help you and protect you. Start with who this guy is, what he did to you, and why you think he's coming after you?" Mike said to her.

"Let her sit down," Jack said and helped her to the edge of the bed.

"I think we all need to get comfortable. I don't expect you to leave anything out. Understand?" Jack asked, looking angry and firm. She nodded her head as she took the seat and clasped her fingers.

"I used to live in Connecticut," she said and hesitated.

"We know that, and that you don't have any family. Get to the part about the guy," Mike said, arms still crossed. Danny and Jack looked at him.

"Don't get all interrogator, cop mode. Give her a time to get it out," Danny told his brother.

Marlena swallowed hard and began to explain about being an accountant and working for a company and how she met Peter.

"That's the dick's name?" Jack asked.

"Peter what?" Mike asked.

"Why do you have to know?" she asked.

"So we can make sure he doesn't come anywhere near what's ours," Jack said before Mike could.

They looked so upset with her already. How could she tell them what Peter did to her?

"Go on, honey, explain," Danny said and placed his hand over hers, gave them a squeeze for encouragement, and then pulled back.

"It's embarrassing," she said.

"Don't be embarrassed. Talk to us," Jack said.

"I want to, but you're older and more experienced and you'll think I was so stupid and naive, which I was, but I know better now. I figured it out when it was too late."

"Figured what out?" Danny asked. She looked at him and held his gaze.

"That Peter was using me for his own purpose. He was showing me off. Making demands on me then putting me down in front of people. He would build me up and make me feel like I was loved and cared for when we were alone but then he became abusive and rough."

"He hit you?" Jack asked, eyes squinting.

"Yes. But mostly he was verbally abusive and tried breaking down my confidence and controlling me. I was only twenty-two when I met him and fell for his charms, his good looks, and powerful demeanor."

"He's a rich asshole?" Mike asked.

She nodded her head.

"When did you break things off with him? Why do you think he's after you?" Mike pushed to get to the point and she was shaking as the tears filled her eyes.

"I broke things off when I realized he was cheating on me. He attacked me one night and got crazy. He threatened me, bruised my ribs, and struck me several times. He left me at a party looking like a piece of used trash. I went to the police and got an order of protection against him. I explained how he assaulted me and he got someone to say he was with them that it wasn't me and that I was lying because I was a worthless whore."

"Jesus, what a fucking prick," Danny said and caressed her thigh.

"What happened next? You took off and wound up here?" Mike asked. She shook her head.

"I was home alone in my apartment. I was trying to figure out where to go and how to get out of town, when I started smelling smoke. I usually put a little something in the oven, but I wasn't very hungry. Peter knew I would do that. Come home and make a dinner, even a small one just for me. But that night I put on the stove for soup. I walked out of the kitchen and heard a noise and a fire broke out. It was so quick, and obvious by the way it immediately spread around the apartment that some kind of accelerant or wiring was used. I was caught inside. I tried to get to the door but I couldn't. There were flames everywhere. I didn't know what to do because I was on the tenth floor. There were no fire escapes on my side by my windows. I grabbed the small fire extinguisher and ran to the bathroom, turned on the shower and the faucet to fill the tub, thinking I could throw water on the flames and use the extinguisher to hold off the flames until the firefighters came.

"I could hear the sirens in the distance and everything. I knew help was coming but the flames were shooting into the bathroom. I felt the pain and heat against my side as the sparks of flame hit my hip and I was on fire. I hopped into the tub, grabbed the curtain and the fire extinguisher. I sprayed at the flames with the extinguisher and screamed out for help until firefighters got there. They place was destroyed and they were shocked to see me in the tub and with the extinguisher. I should have died in there. That's what Peter wanted. He set that fire. But the police, the firefighters couldn't prove anything."

"Oh Jesus, baby, that's the scar on your hip?" Jack asked, kneeling down next to her and caressing her hip. She nodded her head.

"The detectives and arson investigators couldn't prove arson?" Mike asked.

"They proved the cause was arson and there was an investigation, but Peter had an alibi once again. A woman. The one he cheated on me with."

"I don't understand it. The arson investigators, the detectives would have pushed passed some bogus alibi to get the truth." Mike raised his voice.

Marlena stood up. "You think I'm lying? You think I'm making this up? *This* up?" she repeated and pushed down her shorts, raised her top, and revealed the scar from the burn she had gotten. Tears rolled down her cheeks.

"Get out! All of you, now," she yelled. She was so angry she was shaking. But the three men didn't move.

"I said get out!" she yelled again as tears rolled down her cheeks.

"No, Marlena. We're not getting out. You're not pushing us away. We care about you," Danny told her and stepped forward and pulled her into his arms. She felt the hands on her back rubbing her.

"We asked for the truth and you told us. We're not going to lie to you. We're pissed off, we're concerned, and things are going to change around here whether you like it or not," Jack said.

She pulled back, looking at Danny, who held her, reached up, and caressed the tears from her eyes.

Then she looked at Jack. "What do you mean?" she asked.

Mike stepped closer but didn't touch her. She felt sick. He didn't want her because of what Peter did to her. What she allowed him to take from her.

"He means that you're our woman. We're claiming you officially with the sheriff, tonight. We're going to protect you, be with you, and provide for you. No more holding back. No lies. No keeping things from us out of fear that we'll be angry or that we could get hurt or some other nonsense bullshit. You understand me?" Mike asked her.

She sniffled and could hardly hold his gaze, her eyes were tearing so much.

"You don't hate me?" she asked him.

Mike uncrossed his arms and Danny and Jack released her to him.

"Goddamn, baby, no fucking way do I hate you. I'm practically in love with you if you would let the damn wall down now and let us in. You need us. You're ours, and there are no more arguments about it anymore. Got it?" he asked, pulling her hard up against his chest.

She nodded her head and wrapped her arms around his shoulders.

"Are you sure, Mike?" she whispered.

"As sure as anything." He leaned down and kissed her deeply. She let herself go. She gave her all in that kiss and then felt Mike lift her up and lay her down on the bed. He eased up slightly, his one thigh between her legs as he stared down into her eyes.

"You're not going anywhere. You belong with my brothers and me. And when you're not working, you'll be with one of us. Making love, letting us possess every part of you in every way. You got it?" he asked. She felt her heart racing and her belly quiver with excitement and love.

She looked at all three of them as they gathered around her on the bed. Jack was unbuttoning his shirt while Danny was pulling his up and over his head.

"What are you doing?" she whispered, even though she knew what they were doing and what she wanted. Them.

Naked and making love to her for the rest of the night. Forever.

"Getting ready to possess you in every way. To care for you, to make love to you, and to have your heart and your soul like you already have ours," Jack said.

She smiled then bit her lower lip.

"I've never been with three men before. Uhm…will it hurt?" she asked shyly.

Danny smiled and the clapped his hands together and rubbed them.

"Only a little when I slap that ass while I'm fucking it."

"Danny," Mike and Jack scolded.

Marlena gulped. "Oh God. I don't know about this," she said.

"Nice and slow, Marlena. We've got all the time in the world. Forever in fact," Jack said then leaned over and began to lift up her tank top. Mike slid off the bed and discarded his clothing. Jack pushed her shorts and panties down, and Danny moved in to take a taste. His head was between her legs in no time and she was naked, holding his head, and feeling already ready to explode.

She rocked her hips and titled her head back until she caught sight of Jack and Mike naked. Her mouth watered and she reached out to touch them. But they had different ideas and so did Danny.

Danny lifted up and smiled. "Fucking delicious." He gripped her hips, flipped her over then pulled her back.

"Condoms?" he said aloud.

"Right here," Jack said, passing him one.

She shivered and shook, she was so aroused. She couldn't help but wonder if he would take her ass. She wanted them everywhere. She wanted to be their possession, their woman.

She didn't want anything between them as she looked over her shoulder to see Danny fumbling with the condom. Jack caressed her back and ass, and Mike watched her with sultry eyes. He leaned over and cupped her breasts.

"You don't need the condoms. I'm on the pill. I'm clean. I always used protection with Peter." Danny threw the condom and gripped her hips, pulling them back and against him.

He lay over her back softly and kissed her neck, and whispered into her ear.

"Never say his name in our bed, when we're making love. He's gone. He doesn't exist with us. We're your lovers. Your only ones."

"Yes," she said and closed her eyes.

She felt her legs being spread wide and then Danny's mouth on her cunt from behind. He pressed his tongue in and out as Jack touched her cheek and brought his cock to her mouth.

She didn't hesitate as she took it between her lips and began to suck his cock. Back and forth, she bobbed her head until she felt

Danny lifting her higher. Mike slid underneath. They moved her around how they liked and easily with their big muscles and strong capabilities. It aroused her as she came just as Danny thrust fingers to her cunt.

"Oh, she's ready for us," Danny said to them. She felt his tongue lick back and forth over her crevice. The she felt his fingers again thrust into her cunt then back over her puckered hole. A moment later she felt Mike's cock as he gripped her hips and held her gaze.

"You want us?" She nodded as she moaned, still sucking Jack's cock as he held her hair and caressed her cheek. She took in all the sounds, the smells, and the sensations. Men's cologne, soap, masculinity, and control. She wanted to please them, to give them every part of her and just let go. She wanted them in her life forever. She wanted their love, their touches, and their bodies. She moaned louder as cream dripped from her cunt.

"Fuck, she's coming like crazy. She's so turned on," Danny said.

"Then she's ready. She ready for all of us," Mike said and then she felt his cock against her pussy. She moaned against Jack's cock.

"Get inside of her. I'm not going to last long," he said, and then Mike pushed upward and she cried out from the fast penetration. She let him hold her hips and rock up into her as Jack held her head to steady her as he fucked her mouth. She was overwhelmed with emotions and need. Then she felt the finger press into her anus and she lost it. She shook and shivered but the three men had plans. She let go. She let them have complete control as the tears rolled down her face and happiness filled her heart. She felt Danny's fingers pull from her ass and she thrust her ass backward in resistance to him leaving their position. But then she felt the thick, bulbous head of his cock and heard his calm, deep voice against her ear and neck. It sent shivers and vibrations through her body.

"I'm coming in. We're yours and you're ours. Tonight is only the beginning, baby." He slowly pushed into her and she couldn't breathe. Jack kept pumping and Mike held her steady, his cock deep in her cunt. Then she felt Danny ease in and out until she felt the pop and he sunk all the way into her ass. They all moaned and took a moment to just feel the sensations of being inside of her.

"Move. Fucking move. I'm there," Jack complained. In and out, they thrust into her in sync.

"Marlena, I'm coming, baby. Let me out if you don't want to swallow," Jack said. She was touched that he offered. Peter never had. He forced her to swallow him even when she didn't even want to give him oral sex. He was a jerk. These men were different. They seemed to really care and want her.

She held him steady as he grunted and came. She swallowed all of him until he pulled from her mouth and reprimanded her for torturing him.

Then Mike and Danny took over. The bed rocked and moaned, the moans filling the room as their bodies slapped against one another. She loved them. She knew it, and after tonight there was no turning back.

Marlena felt her body tighten up just as Danny roared his release and shoved balls-deep into her ass. He shook and shivered, then gave her ass a series of five smacks. She creamed some more. He pulled out slowly, kissing her spine and caressing her ass until Mike took over complete control. He rolled her to her back and thrust into her hard and fast. Their fingers clasped together as he raised them above her head and rocked into her. Their gazes locked.

"Ours forever. Never anyone else."

"Never," she said and then let go as her body convulsed one more time along with Mike. They came together then he held her in his arms, promising her protection, compassion, and ultimately more than anyone had ever offered her in her life.

* * * *

Mike held Marlena in his arms. Her breasts were pressed up against his chest as Jack pressed up behind her. Jack's hand caressed her outer thigh and up to where the burn on her skin from the fire sat. It was the same side she had the blisters on from the cup of coffee Vicky pushed on her. It pissed him off. He hadn't wanted Marlena to feel any pain. Never again. Not as long as he were alive.

He inhaled her shampoo and the scent of their lovemaking in the air. Jack sat in a chair, half-dressed with his legs stretched out on the bottom of the bed. They were all around her. Their lovemaking so intense, so deep, he actually felt fearful.

He swallowed hard as he stared at the discoloration on her skin, and thought about the fear she had to have had when she was caught in the horrible fire. A fire her boyfriend set to try and kill her. He needed to talk with Max. The sheriff and some of their other close friends who had experience and connections in law enforcement and the government would know what to do. He and his brothers would protect her forever.

When he ran a finger gently along the raised skin, she flinched and nonchalantly moved onto her back so he couldn't touch her there. It was obvious she was sensitive. She crossed her arms to try and cover her large breasts but she was unsuccessful.

"Baby, don't even try it. They're way too beautiful to cover up," Jack said as he reached over and cupped a breast. He lowered his mouth to her lips, kissed her, and then her breast.

Mike turned onto his side and ran his hand along her belly. He played with the small delicate decoration, a diamond hoop. It was feminine and petite like her.

She giggled and reached out to caress the top of his hand.

"Jack," she moaned as Jack suckled her breast and pulled on the nipple. Mike eased his hand between her legs and softly caressed her mound.

The bed dipped.

"Open for us. Offer us what's ours, Marlena," Danny told her.

Danny was once again naked and between her legs, stroking a finger into her cunt, making her moan and thrust. She tried to push her legs together, but Mike and Jack pressed them wider with their palms. Mike leaned down and licked across her nipple.

"Your body is amazing, Marlena. Every inch of you is gorgeous," he said and then leaned up and kissed her.

"Hold her for me. Put her hands above her head. I want to see her breasts bounce so sexy, and her eyes dilate while I make her come again and again," Danny said and Mike and Jack massaged up each arm and then pressed them high above her head.

"Oh God please, Danny. I'm shaking."

Danny sat up between her spread thighs that Mike and Jack held open with their other hand. Danny stroked his cock, letting the tip tap against Marlena's pussy lips.

"Oh," she moaned.

"That's because you need cock. Our cocks inside of you. Isn't that right?" he asked her then pressed the tip of his cock slightly into her pussy.

"Yes. Yes, I do."

"That's right." He reached up and cupped both breasts, bringing them together and massaging them.

"How do you want us, Marlena? One at a time or together, with a cock in every hole?" he asked.

"Oh. My. God," she said and shook as she came.

"Eyes open. Look at us as you come," Danny ordered. Her eyes popped open and Mike felt his own cock harden. He was totally turned on by this. By sharing Marlena with his brothers, his best friends.

"I need her, too," Mike said and then stroked along her pussy, being sure not to touch his brother's cock.

"Yes, Mike. Yes. However you want me. I don't care just take me. All of you," she said and Danny chuckled.

"Oh, we plan on it. Again, and again, and again."

Jack lay down on the edge of the bed with his legs lying over the side. Danny lifted her up and placed her onto Jack, who pressed his cock immediately up into her wet cunt. They both moaned.

"I have her mouth this time. I want to feel those sexy lips on me. You get her sexy ass," Danny said and gave her ass a slap as he got into position.

Mike got into position behind her as he stood on the rug and caressed her ass.

"Pull out a sec, bro, I need to get this ass ready for me," Mike said and Jack lifted her up by the hips, pulling his cock from her pussy. Mike pressed fingers to her cunt from behind and stroked her over and over again, until she was panting and creaming everywhere. He stroked fingers over her anus then pressed one in. "We're good," he said as he used his other hand to massage her ass. Jack pulled her down for a kiss and thrust his cock up into her pussy, making her moan and thrust against him.

She cried out when Jack released her lips and started thrusting hard and fast upward. Then Danny took her face between his hands and kissed her deeply as Mike fingered her ass, getting it ready. Mike couldn't take it anymore. He wanted in. He wanted to claim her ass, claim every part of her, every inch, and mark her his woman. He would protect her and watch over her always.

He pulled his fingers from her ass and replaced them with his cock. He slowly pushed through the tight rings and Marlena moaned and bucked on top of Jack.

"I've got something for you, Marlena. Come on now and be a good girl," Danny said and pressed his cock to her lips. She must have opened immediately because Danny moaned and then it was on. They worked their cocks into her together, making her moan and thrust. Mike slapped her ass, massaged the cheeks, then smacked her ass again. He could feel her cream drip and then heard Danny grunt as he came and Jack followed. Mike thrust harder, faster, wanting, needing to mark her so she knew she would never belong to anyone but them and then he heard her scream her orgasm and he couldn't hold back. He grunted and called out her name as he came.

"Marlena! Marlena!"

He held himself within her and caught his breath. He stared at the marking on her hip and he caressed it, held her hips despite her shifting and trying to still pull away. He pulled her back as Jack and Danny released her and he hugged her back to his chest.

"Don't hold back and be afraid. He can't hurt you anymore. We'll protect you. Just trust us," he said and kissed her shoulder. He felt her ease up and relax as he slowly pulled from her body. Jack was there with a washcloth for her, and as he caressed her skin, Jack kissed her. Mike locked gazes with Danny, and his brother didn't have to say a word. Tomorrow they would start the hunt. Tomorrow they would take the steps to ensure Marlena was safe in Chance and with them, forever.

Chapter 8

"I can't be late for work," Marlena said, stepping out of the shower and wrapping a towel around her body. Danny watched as he stood in the doorway with his arms crossed in front of his bare chest. His brothers had left for work earlier. Every day this week they stayed the night at Marlena's place. But last night, after they all made love and as she slept, they awoke hearing her crying and moaning in her sleep. He wanted to ask her about it and wondered if it was a normal occurrence. Could she be having nightmares of the fire and not telling them?

"Why are you looking at me like that?" she asked, pulling the towel from her body and wrapping her hair in it. She flipped her head over then used the towel to wrap around her head before placing it on top. He was always amazed about how women did that, but with Marlena he watched her every move. He wanted to memorize every detail, every marking on her body from the scar that made him long to hurt the man responsible, to every pretty, dainty freckle and beauty mark.

She was stunning, and she was theirs.

"I'm not allowed to look at you? To admire your sexy body, and think about the many ways I want to explore it with my brothers?" he teased. Her cheeks turned a nice shade of red and she quickly stepped into her tiny black thong and a crisp white bra she had to stuff her breast into.

He licked his lips. He adored her body, her beauty, her everything.

Marlena took the towel off her head, towel-dried her hair, then ran a brush through the long blond strands.

She bent over to reach under the counter for the hair dryer, like she did every morning this week, and he uncrossed his arms, snagged her around the waist, and held her to him.

"Danny," she scolded, gripping onto his forearms. But he held her gaze in the reflection of the mirror and she smiled and leaned back against his chest.

He ran his palm along her belly, over the gold hoop and then kissed her neck. "You smell edible."

"You always tell me that, even when I smell like diner food," she retorted. He chuckled and he felt her shiver from the warm breath against her skin.

"That's good. You know I can eat you up any time of the day." He trailed a finger down her belly to her panties and cupped her mound. She gripped his wrist.

"Daniel Spencer, I've got to get to work. Alice is going to be mad and your parents will wonder what's going on."

She pressed his hand away and he stepped back, swatting her ass before he took a seat on the closed lid of the toilet and watched her.

"No they won't. Everyone knows that you're with us." She turned a nice shade of red. He loved doing that to her. Making her blush with dirty talk or things like what he just said. She was shy, reserved, and as they learned more about her life, they learned about how hard she had it. No family, no guidance, and one manipulative man she saw as a savior, a hero to whisk her away from the pain and the struggles in her desperation for love. He used her, manipulated her, and took advantage of her innocence. It wasn't right. She could have died at his hands or in that fire.

He watched her dry her long blonde hair and he couldn't resist reaching out and caressing her bare ass. He ran his fingers along the thong string between her ass cheeks and thought about how he and his brothers got to fuck that ass, and how they took her together almost every time they made love. In a week's time he felt so desperate to make certain she knew that they adored her and wanted her in their lives forever. But she was holding back. Like with the nightmares.

She turned off the hair dryer and then began to fix her hair.

He caressed her hip and she turned to look at him, her arms raised above her head as she fixed her hair.

"Stay like that. God, you look incredible," he whispered then leaned forward and kissed her breasts then lower to her belly.

"Danny, I really need to get dressed."

She lowered her arms and placed them on his shoulders. He hugged her to him and felt her run her fingers through his hair then tilt his head back. She held his gaze.

"I want you to know that I feel it, too. That I would love to not go to work and to stay here and make love to you and your brothers all day long. Just to feel you hold me in your arms makes me smile and makes my life that much better. I want you to know that you, Jack, and Mike mean so much to me. I trust you. I want to be with you. But I have to work and make money to support myself."

He smiled then kissed her lips.

"That makes me very happy. I'm glad you trust us." He gave her ass a tap and then turned her around and gave her a gentle push toward the door.

"Hurry up and get dressed, or I'll forget what you just said, tear those panties from that body, and have my way with you."

She looked at him and he raised one of his eyebrows up at her. She quickly hurried from the room. She knew he was serious.

He waited a moment and took a deep breath. Danny had never felt like this about anyone. Ever. He adored her. Hell, he loved her. He needed to talk with Mike and Jack. They could move her into their place. They could have her quit working or maybe work less hours at the diner so they could have more time together. They needed to make plans for their future.

As he exited the bathroom and then walked into her room, he saw that she was dressed in her uniform. Tight black skirt. The short one. White blouse and comfortable white sneakers. She looked incredible.

She was buttoning up the blouse when he approached. He moved her hands and finished buttoning it for her.

"Marlena, can I ask you something?"

"Sure," she said and then walked to the dresser, pulled out lip gloss, and applied it to her lips. She wore hardly any makeup and she didn't need to. She was youthful, sexy, and naturally stunning. Too perfect for the likes of him and his brothers. He was shocked at the thought. Now suddenly his age was getting in the way.

"At night, when we're sleeping, you moan and cry. It's like you're having a bad dream but you don't wake up from it."

She stopped what she was doing and stared at him.

She took an unsteady breath and he wondered if she would lie, or minimize what he knew was a problem, a struggle for her.

"I've been dealing with it for months. Since the fire. It's no big deal," she said and grabbed her small backpack and her car keys.

He took hold of her wrist and reached up and cupped her cheek.

"It is a big deal if you're scared. I'm here for you. So are Mike and Jack."

She hesitated a moment. "I know you are. That's why I've let you stay with me at night. I need you holding me. It makes them less scary." She leaned up and kissed him then headed out of the room.

He was shocked at her response. Relieved and kind of proud. But he still worried. She didn't need to live with that kind of fear and concern. He wanted to take those dreams away forever. He just needed to figure out how.

* * * *

Marlena was in a great mood. She'd never felt so happy and almost at peace. She thought about the conversation she had with

Danny this morning. Her nightmares weren't so terrible or violent with him, Mike, and Jack holding her in their arms at night. In fact, she didn't even wake up screaming and crying from them.

As she placed the order down in front of one of the locals, she heard the bell chime and looked up. Her heart caught in her chest. Her mouth gaped open and she felt almost faint. *Detective Morgan. What is he doing here?*

He read her face and gave a nod then took a seat at the corner table in the back clearly away from any eavesdroppers. She reached for the cup of coffee to bring over to another gentleman and it shook in her hand. She set it down.

"You feeling okay, Marlena? You look a little pale, honey," Mr. Walker, who had a truck delivery business, asked.

"I'm fine. A little too much coffee this morning," she said.

He smiled. "Maybe I shouldn't have this second cup," he teased but took the cup and immediately brought it to his lips and smiled.

She smiled, too, then wiped her hands on her apron and headed over to the detective's table. But not before noticing Roy looking at her and the man in the corner. Detective Morgan stood out like a sore thumb.

"Good afternoon, sir, welcome to Spencer's. What can I get you?"

He looked her over and gave a soft smile then glanced at the menu. He looked around them and then leaned forward.

"You look good, Marlena. I had a hard time finding you."

"How did you?" she whispered.

"It's my job to. Can you sit a minute?"

She pushed a strand of hair behind her ear.

"I don't think so. I wouldn't want to draw too much attention to us. Why are you here? Is something wrong?"

"We need to talk. It's about Peter."

She felt the tears reach her eyes and she pulled out the chair and took a seat. She leaned closer.

"What is it? What's going on?"

"The woman, Maria, that Peter had as an alibi for the fire at your place—she turned up dead last week."

"He killed her?" she asked and covered her mouth with her hand.

He nodded his head then leaned closer. "We've got men, detectives trying to track him down. When we raided his place looking for him, we found stuff. Evidence that links him to the fire at your place."

"Oh God. That's good then. You can find him, catch him, and arrest him for trying to kill me and for killing his girlfriend."

"If we can find him. Marlena, there were things there. We found some upsetting stuff.

"Upsetting stuff?" she asked and then heard the bell ring. She had to bring the orders out. People were waiting for more coffee or refills on drinks.

"I have to get the orders out."

"We need to talk. It's important, Marlena. You're in danger."

She stood up and swallowed hard.

"I get off at four. We can meet out back and talk."

"Okay. I'll be back then."

She stood up and so did he.

"You should order something so it doesn't look suspicious."

He smiled and winked. "No wonder it was so hard to find you. You're right. I'll take a coffee to start."

She headed away and continued working, worrying about what the detective found and also worrying about how to tell her men about him.

But that problem seemed to be taken care of for her. Ten minutes later, Mike, Jack, and Danny entered the diner along with Sheriff Gordon and Taylor Dawn.

Danny headed straight toward her, pulled her into his arms, and held her tight.

"Is the stranger Peter?" he asked, and she shook her head. He looked at his brothers and the sheriff.

"Who is he?" Mike asked.

Detective Morgan stood up. He pushed his dress jacket aside and all the men placed their hands on their guns. "Easy. I'm a detective," Morgan said and showed them his badge.

"From Connecticut?" the sheriff asked, approaching with caution.

"Yes, sheriff. I just got into town to see Marlena, then I was heading to talk with you."

"Why is that?" Mike asked.

Detective Morgan looked at Marlena and she slowly approached.

"He was assigned to my case back in Connecticut. He was the one who told me to disappear because they couldn't prove anything against Peter and how he tried to kill me," Marlena told them.

"What's going on?" Roy asked and he placed his hands on Marlena's shoulders and Rita and Regan joined them, too.

Everyone stared at Detective Morgan. He took a deep breath and released it.

"Marlena is in danger. I've been trying to find her for several weeks. Someone ran a check on the fire in Connecticut. I was tipped off."

"That would be us. We were trying to figure out a full name to this Peter guy who tried to kill Marlena. We take care of our own around here. If she's in danger then we need to know everything," Sheriff Gordon told the detective.

"Then I suggest we all sit down and go over what I have. There's no telling how close Peter could be to finding Marlena, but he's pretty damn resourceful. And if I was tipped off about the calls and interest into the fire at Marlena's apartment, then someone might have tipped off Peter. That's why I headed out here right away. He's got money, and he has connections. Someone is definitely keeping him well hidden, and knowing about what we found in his apartment, the man won't stop until Marlena is dead."

* * * *

Marlena washed up in the back bathroom of the diner. She held on to the sink and stared at her reflection in the mirror. She was overwhelmed with emotions. News spread fast about Marlena being in trouble and the place erupted in support. Adele, Alicia, and Mercedes were there, plus the Ferguson men, the Dawn men, the sheriff, and townspeople, and even Parker, and some of the locals who owned the stores in town.

Mike wasn't kidding when he told her that she had the protection of the people of Chance and that they were pretty damn resourceful.

She closed her eyes as the tears flowed. Never in her entire life, even for a moment, had she experienced such love and compassion. Never.

The door creaked open."

"Marlena, are you okay?" She heard Rita's voice and she nodded her head but didn't turn around.

"Aww, baby. It's going to be all right. My sons, the sheriff, all of us are here for you and will protect you from that bad man," Rita said.

Marlena had told the crowd thank you, but she was overwhelmed as they all remained there while the detective told them about Peter, where they thought he might be, and what evidence they had to prove he was after Marlena. There had been pictures, and he even described what he planned on doing to her to make her suffer. All the people were affected by the information and all of them vowed to protect her. It was too much.

"Why are you hiding in here, when everyone is out there worried about you?"

"I needed a minute," Marlena said and wiped her eyes and then turned toward Rita. The woman smiled softly at her as she caressed her arm.

"You're a strong, brave young woman, and you're perfect for my sons. They love you, and I know you love them."

A tear rolled down her cheek.

"But I don't want to place them, the town, you, and Roy and Regan in danger. I love your sons. I would do anything to protect them."

"And they love you."

Marlena nodded her head and wiped her eyes again.

"Now, straighten out your shoulders, hold your head high, and be strong, like you have been. This man can't have you. He can't take you from us, from Chance. You remember that, and you help the detectives, the sheriff, Mike, and the others to get this guy before he even steps into town. Okay?"

"Yes, ma'am."

Rita pulled her into a hug and Marlena lost it all over again.

"If I had a daughter, I would want her to be as beautiful and as strong as you, Marlena. You're family. You're stuck with us, so get used to it." She gave her shoulders a squeeze then wiped her own tear from her eye before walking out of the bathroom and through the kitchen.

Marlena took a deep breath and wiped her sweaty hands on her apron. She could do this. She could accept their help, their love and protection. Everything would work out fine, and Peter wouldn't hurt any of them. If he did, then she would disappear and make Peter follow her so no one else got hurt. She'd face that fight if and when she had to. There weren't any other options.

Marlena entered the kitchen to see Jack standing there with his arms crossed in front of his chest. He looked her over and he opened his arms wide. She practically ran into them and hugged him tight. The scent of his cologne, the feel of his strong, muscular arms gave her a feeling of instant protection and love.

He ran his hands along her back up and down and then kissed her forehead as she look up into his eyes, her head as far back as nearly her shoulders.

"We're going to stop by the cottage and grab what you need. We're going to bring you to our place. We have a security system in place and one of us will be with you at all times until this guy is located and found. Understand?" he asked in a firm tone that totally told her not to even think about arguing.

She parted her lips and he challenged her with one raised eyebrow and a firm expression. She bit her bottom lip.

"Is that necessary?"

"No room for discussion, and yes. It is," he said. He seemed pretty upset. Had she missed something more when she escaped to the back bathroom for an emotional reprieve?

"Jack, is something wrong? Did Detective Morgan divulge more information?"

"He did privately, between Mike, Danny, and the sheriff and me. We'll talk about it later. Right now plans are being made and the town is being placed on alert. That dick even considers coming here, we'll know about it and take him out before he even gets close to you."

He took her hand and brought it to his lips and kissed her knuckles. Then they headed out of the kitchen and almost everyone was gone. She sighed in relief. She hadn't realized that she didn't want to face them again. It was a combination of embarrassment and admiration.

She glanced at Mike, who was talking with Detective Morgan and the Sheriff, along with Taylor. Alicia, Adele, and Mercedes were there and the second they saw her they approached.

"How are you doing, honey? Hanging in there?" Mercedes asked and drew her in for a hug. Alicia hugged her next and then Adele.

"I'm okay. I just want this over with."

"I'm sure you do. This town is amazing, the way everyone has come together to help," Alicia said.

"They put everyone on high alert and all women must be escorted around town and even on the outskirts until this situation is resolved," Adele added.

"Is that normal protocol?" Marlena asked Jack. He placed his hand on her shoulder.

"Yes. It's how things are done here. Protecting the women of Chance is priority and we especially take these precautions when one is in danger like this," Jack told them.

"Is it really necessary for every woman to be escorted and watched over?" Mercedes asked.

"It sure is. Men are being assigned as we speak," Taylor said, joining them.

Marlena watched how Mercedes locked gazes with Taylor and then looked away.

"In fact, I'll be walking you back to the sheriff's department, Mercedes. So if you're done here, we should head back now," Taylor told her.

"But Marlena needs me," Mercedes said.

Taylor was firm in his response.

"You'll come with me now. Marlena has her men to watch over her and some additional plans to make."

"I guess I don't have much of a choice and need a babysitter," Mercedes said with attitude and then hugged Marlena.

"Be nice," Marlena whispered to her and Mercedes's cheeks turned a nice shade of pink. Mercedes definitely liked Taylor, and it was obvious Taylor liked her but did his brothers, too?

As Mercedes said good-bye, the front door to the diner opened. Leo Ferguson was there and shook hands with everyone as he entered, but his eyes landed on Adele.

"There you are. Looks like my brothers and I will be your personal escorts for a while. How about we head back to the office and then I'll drive you home?" he said to Adele.

"I'm okay. This isn't necessary," Adele said, appearing a bit nervous.

"It's protocol, Adele. We've been assigned to you," he said and she looked at Marlena and hugged her.

"Just cooperate. It isn't a bad thing," Marlena whispered.

"What for, they were 'assigned' to me. Wonderful."

"I'm sorry," Marlena whispered and Alicia hugged Adele and then stood by Marlena.

"Well, we should have lots to talk about tomorrow after this," Alicia teased, and Marlena nodded her head.

"They're going to be pissed at me. I can't believe that everyone has been assigned protectors."

"Not me," Alicia said and smiled.

"Alicia." Marlena and Alicia looked up to see the sheriff standing there.

"Can you come with me please?"

"Oh my God, Alicia, the sheriff?" Marlena whispered as she hugged her.

"Help me, Marlena. He's scary."

"Don't be silly. You're a grown woman. You can handle him."

"That's what you think." Alicia waved good-bye to Mike, Danny, and Jack then met the sheriff by the door.

"We'll be in touch later on," the sheriff said as he held the door open for Alicia, who looked scared out of her mind. Her friends might be freaking out about who their assigned protectors were, but Marlena had a feeling all those men had interest in her friends long before today. Maybe something good would come out of this. Maybe her friends would find true love, and men that could truly care for them and love them. Maybe.

* * * *

Mike couldn't get the images out of his head. Peter Jones was one sick son of a bitch. He tortured and killed his girlfriend then left her for dead. Detective Morgan shared the information they had on Peter so far and about other possible crimes he committed, including the arson at Marlena's apartment building. He also sent along pictures of the evidence and plans the detectives found in Peter's apartment in regards to Marlena. Peter was obsessed with her, and obsessed with the fact that she survived the fire and got away. He wanted her dead.

He felt the hands on his shoulders and he gripped them tight, bringing Marlena around and onto his lap. It was an instinctual move. He heard someone approach, smelled her shampoo, and knew it was her.

She gasped and held onto him. Her long blonde hair flowed over his shoulder and he stared into her eyes. She was so beautiful, so sweet, and didn't deserve the things that monster wanted to do to her.

"Mike?" she whispered and he shook his head, pulled her closer, and kissed her.

That kiss grew deeper, wilder, until she maneuvered over him, straddled his waist, and began to rock her hips.

He ran his hands up under her T-shirt then toward the front and her breasts. He massaged and pulled on her breasts, making her moan into his mouth.

He unclipped the front clasp, pulled from her mouth, and pushed her T-shirt and bra up over her head and off of her. She was now straddling his body, half naked on the back porch of their home. He cupped her breasts and leaned forward to lick the tip of one. She ran her fingers through his hair and continued to rock her hips.

He released the nipples and licked the cleavage to feast on her other breasts. He felt so needy. He wanted to be inside of her, fucking her, making her moan and scream his name.

In the distance the smell of rain approached, the thunder rolled, and lighting struck. The night sky grew darker as the storm rolled in and it matched the same storm brewing inside of his body. He lifted her up to stand and unzipped her jeans, shoving them and her panties down her thighs. She ran her hands along his pectoral muscles then leaned forward to lick a nipple. He undid his own pants, shoved them down, then lifted her up to straddle him. Painstakingly he maneuvered, without tripping, toward the wall. He pressed her hard against it.

"I can't hold back. I can't get you to a bed."

She shook her head.

"Here. Take me right here in the storm, in your arms, against your house. Any way you want me."

The thunder rolled again and the lightning struck just as he aligned his cock with her wet pussy and thrust upward. They both cried out and he began to thrust his hips, stroke his cock deeper into her cunt as she held on tight.

"More, Mike. I need you. All of you. Harder," she begged, and he gave her what she asked for. He took what he needed to and thrust hard and fast into her, trying to reach that feeling of satisfaction and ultimate possession. Her breasts pressed against his chest. Her lips seared his neck, his ear, and then his lips.

"I love you, Mike," she whispered.

"Fuck." He roared and gripped her hips and banged into her hard. So hard she leaned back against the wall, covered his hands with hers, and held his gaze.

"Take me. Claim all of me," she said. Her breasts were fully exposed and rocking up and down with his deep, hard thrusts. She looked so damn sexy and vulnerable and he knew he loved her, too.

He closed his eyes and continued to thrust into her as the thunder struck, the lightning illuminated the porch, and flashes of the gruesome cruel images of Peter's plans scattered through his mind.

"Marlena, I love you," he said and she cried out her release. He pulled her close and let his body go as he held on tight and came inside of her.

"I love you, baby. You're safe here in these arms. You're safe."

"I know I am. I know, Mike. I know."

* * * *

Marlena lay in Mike's arms on the lounge chair on the porch. She was getting cold, now that the rain was coming down. The wind blew and cascaded water over them, making her gasp and Mike chuckle.

"Let's get you inside," he said and scooped her up into his arms. He reached for the door but Danny was there. He smiled.

"We were wondering when you two were going to come in."

Danny's eyes swept over Marlena's breasts as Mike carried her inside.

She saw Jack go toward the door. She heard it slam closed and then a few seconds later slam closed again. Then the doors locked and the alarm was set.

Mike carried her up the stairs to their bedroom. Their house was stunning and so big. Too big for three men to live in alone. When they carried her to the room they called the guest bedroom, she was shocked. It was stunning and had a large king-size bed and looked welcoming.

"I love this bed. It looks so big and fluffy," she said and Mike lifted her up and dropped her onto the bed. She screamed and then he tickled her and climbed on top of her. He pressed her arms up and above her head so her breasts stuck out.

"This is a nice comfortable bed, where my brothers and I can spread you out and make wild, passionate love to you," he told her as he held her gaze and slowly leaned down closer.

His nose tickled her skin along with his warm breath as he teased her.

She giggled.

"Now where should I taste first?" he asked, pretending to go to her left breast then back to her right breast and then he struck his tongue out and suckled against the sensitive part of her neck that had her wiggling and screaming for mercy.

She tilted her pelvis up and tried to get free, but it was no use. Mike was huge and muscular and could easily overpower her. He continued to lick and suckle her skin until she felt the bed dip.

"Our turn to enjoy our woman's body," Danny said, and Mike lifted her up, his cock hard and long against her belly.

He winked, and caressed her calves and her thighs, and then he pulled her down lower to the edge of the bed. He flipped her onto her belly and massaged her ass.

"Lay still. The fun is about to begin." He gave her ass a light smack and she shivered with anticipation.

Danny took over. He spread her thighs and lifted her hips and she felt his fingers thrust up into her cunt from behind. She felt full and tender as she widened her stance and rocked her hips back against Danny's fingers.

She wanted and needed so desperately. It was crazy. First on the porch in the rain during a thunder and lightning storm and now here with her men surrounding her. It seemed as though she had her own smoldering storm brewing stronger inside of her that needed to be let free.

"Does that feel good, baby?" Danny asked then licked between her ass cheeks and began to move his finger along the crack.

"Yes. Oh God, yes."

"Then this is going to feel even better."

She felt them moving around behind her but her face was against the sheets and her breasts snug against the warm, fluffy comforter. Danny spread her thighs wider and stoked her anus. She felt something cold and thick and then his fingers pressed into her ass.

"It burns, oh it's wet."

"Just like you, sweetness. Danny's going to get that ass ready for cock," Jack told her as he pushed her hair from her cheeks and leaned down to kiss her.

God, his lips felt so good. She felt frantic, needy. It was like each time they had sex it got better and her desire increased.

She lifted up so she could kiss him back and Danny pulled his fingers from her anus and replaced them with his cock. With the cool liquid lubricating her ass, his thick, hard cock slid right in and they both moaned.

She shivered, eyes closed as she relished in the feel of his flesh against hers and their bodies locked in the most intimate way.

"That's it, baby. I love this ass. Fuck, it feels so good. I love that you're here with us. It's where you belong," Danny said and he began to rock his hips. His cock slid in and out of her ass, causing tiny vibrations to erupt in her inner muscles. Suddenly her pussy ached something terrible. It felt swollen and needy as she lifted up and pushed back.

"That's my girl. You like my cock in your ass, fucking you, don't you, love?" Danny asked. That dirty talk drove her insane. Plus his hands were manipulating her ass, her hips, and then her breasts as he reached under her arms and cupped them. It was overwhelming. She felt completely safe, encased by his much larger body. Even his thighs turned her on, and the feel of steel against her outer thighs. She loved it. She loved him.

She could feel his balls slapping against her pussy from behind. It tickled and teased her cunt and made her desperate for penetration there, too.

"Yes. Oh God yes," she said and then maneuvered her fingers between her pussy as she teetered on her knees at the edge of the bed and stroked her own cunt. In and out, she fingered herself while Danny thrust his cock into her ass.

She absorbed every sensation and touch. The way his large hands splayed over her sensitive skin as he gripped her hips and stroked her pussy.

"What are you doing, Marlena?" Mike questioned her in that tone of his as he eased onto the side of the bed. Even that turned her on and made cream drip from her cunt and cause her need to increase another notch.

Her lips were parted and her eyes closed as she felt her pussy get tighter and tighter. Mike's authoritative, demanding tone had a major and instant effect on her body.

"Answer me, Marlena," Mike barked as he ran his hand along her spine to her hair and gave a little tug.

"She's fingering herself, Mike," Jack said and ran his hands up and down her back then over her ass cheeks as Danny slowly stroked his cock into her ass.

She lifted up and pressed her fingers faster, deeper into her cunt, feeling her own cream while the tight, sensitive vibrations erupted inside of her anus.

"Oh, oh," she moaned louder.

"Fuck that's hot. Make yourself come, baby," Danny told her, and he lifted back so she rose up higher. She'd never felt so sensitive as she rocked her hips, fingered her pussy, and let Danny continue to fuck her ass.

She moaned and gasped when Mike pulled on her left nipple and Jack pulled on her right nipple. She pressed a finger to her clit and then pressed in and out of her cunt. She felt wild, needy, and wanted to come. She swirled her fingers around her clit and added pressure then thrust her fingers into her cunt again and again. She panted louder and louder and then Danny shoved his cock balls-deep into her ass as Mike and Jack pulled hard on her nipples. She screamed her release and continued to shake and shiver in the after effects.

Then in a flash, all three men were moving her around to their liking. Jack slid underneath her and Mike cupped her face and hair as he brought his cock to her lips. "Suck it. We want you together. I need your mouth, baby. I'm going to come fast."

He looked wild, desperate, and she knew exactly how he felt. She didn't hesitate as she moved in for a taste of heaven. She wanted to please him. She wanted to make him feel as wild as him and his brothers made her feel, and she would.

Jack slid in underneath her and as she opened wide, Danny pulled slightly out of her ass as Jack thrust upward into her pussy and she accepted Mike's cock into her mouth.

It was overwhelming. She felt frantic, wild, and like some wanton untamed animal in need of cock and a fulfillment only these three men could give her. They moaned and thrust, rocked the bed, caressed her, manipulated her body in a way she never knew existed as she put her own effort into giving them back what they gave her. She sucked Mike's cock diligently, she thrust back against Danny's cock with ease, and then down onto Jack's shaft. It was like some wild out-of-body experience and she didn't know where the coordination, the energy, even came from.

"Fuck, Marlena. I'm coming, baby," Mike yelled out as he gripped her hair and thrust deeper into her mouth. She grabbed onto Jack and sucked Mike until he was pulling out, moaning and panting. Jack took that moment to nip her breast and then grip her hips and shove upward. He came next and she felt her juices begin to flow when Danny held her hips tight and pounded into her ass, calling her name until she screamed her release and then he finally let go and came, too.

It was the most magical experience of her lifetime. She felt sedated, loved, and important. The thought that Peter could ruin it all entered her mind and she hugged Jack tight. Wrapped her arms around his shoulders until he hugged her back and rolled her to the side. He caressed her everywhere until she felt the warm washcloth against her ass then Jack pressing her back so Mike could clean her front.

"I love you guys. You mean more to me than anything else. I would give my life for each of you. I don't want to lose you," she said, and the tears flowed as Jack hugged her to him and Danny and Mike joined them on the bed. She could feel the three of them caressing her and kissing her.

"You're not going to lose us. We're here to protect you and love you, Marlena. Let us do our jobs," Mike said, and she pulled back from Jack and held Mike's gaze.

"I won't let anything happen to the three of you because of Peter."

"Baby, you're not alone anymore. You've got us and the town. You're safe right here with us. Always," Jack told her.

"Come on now, lie down and rest with us. It's been a long day, and tomorrow we'll need to make some plans, now that you're in our protective custody," he teased.

"Protective custody?" she asked.

Danny trailed a finger along her thigh, over her pussy, and then to her breasts, making her giggle and squirm.

"You're our woman and we love you. The three of us protect what's ours. No one will ever get between us, Marlena. No one."

Chapter 9

Marlena was getting used to having one of the guys sitting in the diner as she worked. Although she didn't think it was necessary considering that there were other townsfolk sitting watch, and wearing firearms. She swore it was like something out of an old western instead of South Carolina.

As she made her way over toward the table where Alicia was sitting, she heard her whispering into her cell phone. She seemed really upset.

Marlena whispered to Alicia, trying not to interrupt. "Who is that?"

Alicia rolled her eyes and gave her that expression like "Who do you think?"

Tony.

Marlena never met the jerk, but she knew he had hurt Alicia's feelings, used her in some big job investment, and even cheated on her. He was a wealthy, pompous jerk that Alicia just couldn't seem to get rid of.

"Listen, I need to go. I understand what you're saying, but I don't need your advice. Good-bye." She disconnected the call and Marlena placed her hand on her hip.

"Why do you even accept his phone calls? He's a manipulative jerk," Marlena told her.

Alicia lowered her eyes to her lap. "I don't know. I guess I'm trying to hold on to something in order to not feel like I made a mistake allowing Tony to get so close to me."

"You didn't make a mistake. You were honest and he wasn't. He used you for your money."

"He gave part of it back."

"After you threatened to sue him."

"I know, I know, we've been over this before. It's just so hard because we were friends first."

Marlena felt badly for Alicia. She knew that her and Tony were friends for years and that they talked about getting married. She gave her virginity to the guy and tried to hold onto the fantasy he created for her. But not only did he steal money from Alicia, he also cheated on her with Alicia's best friend at the time. What a mess. Marlena was sure that Alicia hadn't explained everything. It seemed to her that Tony had some invisible hold on Alicia. She wished she could sever it and move on.

"So, how are you holding up with your bodyguards on duty twenty-four-seven?" she asked Marlena and nodded toward the side where Danny sat talking to Monroe Gordon.

Marlena glanced that way and smiled.

She looked at Alicia. "It's not so bad."

"Oh boy, you're in love with them, aren't you?"

She took a deep breath and released it.

"God, it's crazy, but I am."

Alicia smiled.

"I'm so happy for you, Marlena. You deserve this. You deserve to be happy, to have men that love you and can protect you. God, what I would do for a man to love me, to look at me the way Mike, Danny, and Jack look at you." Alicia looked toward Danny and Monroe. Then back at Marlena.

"They eat you up with their eyes. It's amazing to watch."

Marlena glanced toward Monroe and Danny. She noticed Monroe looking over.

"I think you have some admirers of your own, Alicia."

Alicia's eyes widened and then she huffed.

"Are you kidding me? Monroe Gordon is out of my league. He can have his choice of any female anywhere, the way he travels and invests in companies with his brothers."

"Honey, he could be anywhere, even on a private jet flying off somewhere, but he's not. He's here at Rita's, watching over you."

"Oh, he didn't choose to have to be my guardian during this dangerous time. His brother, the mean, irritable, overcommanding sheriff probably forced him into it. I'll tell you one thing, when I had to leave with Sheriff Gordon the other day from here, when you got the news about Peter, I was shaking in my heels. Do you know that man read me the riot act? He talked to me about taking precautions, not going anywhere alone, reaching out to him only if I felt I was in any danger or even scared. God, it was like he thought I had no gut instincts or knowledge of being aware of my surroundings."

Marlena chuckled and Alicia barked at her. "What? Why are you laughing?"

"Because, I've never seen you get so riled up over a man before. It's like the sheriff gets under your skin."

"He rubs me the wrong way."

"You like him, that's what's pissing you off."

"I do not. I definitely don't need another controlling, demanding man in my life telling me what to do and where to go and who to hang out with."

"That's not what the sheriff did."

"Close enough."

Marlena laughed.

"Well, I think you've caught the eyes of all three Gordon brothers. Maybe a little push is exactly what you need."

Marlena heard the bell ring and knew the food orders were up.

"Excuse me while I get back to work." Marlena winked and Alicia shook her head.

"You're the one who found three great men. I'm destined for loneliness, to be a failure, and more than likely have Tony up my you-know-what for the rest of my life because I'm such a scaredy cat when it comes to him."

"The first step in solving a problem is first admitting that you have one. You'll figure it out, and if you can't get rid of him, I know a very tough, sexy deputy that I'm sure would be happy to kick some jerk's ass for you. Mike's been gnawing at the bit for days now."

Alicia chuckled.

Marlena walked away and glanced at Danny. He nodded his head and she turned away.

After work, they would head to her place to get some more clothes. She was upset at not being able to enjoy the new kitchen cabinets they completed. What a shame. All because Peter was on the run from police and possibly heading to find her. But how could he find her? She was all the way in South Carolina. How could he get tipped off?

She delivered the food and went about her work day, swamped as ever. Seemed to her that every person living within the perimeters of Chance decided to pay a visit to meet her, give their word of personal protection, and console her. Chance was a special town indeed. She was beginning to think Peter would never even reach the perimeter of town, never mind get away with standing right in front of her.

It seemed to her more and more that coming here, deciding on staying put in the town with the choice based solely on its name, was the right move after all. Maybe she was getting better at making decisions and following her gut instincts. Having her three new best friends and falling in love with the Spencer brothers were what was keeping her less panicked and more confident. Hopefully the police caught Peter before he even stepped into South Carolina. That was what she really hoped for.

* * * *

Mike and Deputy Taylor Dawn headed to Marlena's cottage to do a drive-by. They knew that the town entrances were covered by patrols and that pictures of Peter Jones were posted and passed around to anyone they could reach. But Mike was antsy and doing the drive-by this late afternoon would make him feel like he was accomplishing something.

As they came up the drive along his uncle's old place, he caught a glimpse of something by the front door.

"You see that?" Taylor asked, catching it, too.

"Shit, look at the side window. Did Marlena leave that open?" Taylor asked.

"I don't think so. We were sure to lock things ups good and tight. Let's be careful," Mike said.

"Should we call it in?"

"Not yet. We don't know what we got. Just be ready," Mike told Taylor.

"You got it, buddy."

They slowly pulled up closer and Mike could see the broken glass.

"Fuck, looks like someone might have broken in."

Mike placed the car in park and turned off the engine.

"I'll take the front. You want to head around back, in case someone is still in there?" Mike asked.

"You got it."

They got out of the car and drew their weapons. They used their training to case the perimeter of the house and slowly approach. Taylor disappeared around back and Mike stepped onto the porch, hearing the old wooden planks creak.

He cursed under his breath.

He slowly turned the front doorknob and it released. The person who broke in probably left through the front door.

He walked inside and could see Taylor making his way in from the back porch.

"All clear," he called out as Mike checked the living room, the kitchen, and then the bedroom.

"All clear."

But the bedroom wasn't neat and tidy like Marlena left it. Instead her clothes were scattered everywhere, the glass on the dresser mirror broken, and a note was left on the bed.

"I'm coming for you," it said in red.

"This is Taylor, I need the sheriff and Detective Morgan to come out to Marlena Courts's place, pronto," Taylor said into his radio, and Mike felt sick to his stomach.

He looked around knowing that Peter, the man who tried to kill his woman, was in here. She would be a mess if she came home to this.

"Shit, I have to call Danny and Jack and tell them not to bring Marlena here. She gets off in thirty minutes. She can't see this. She'll lose it," Mike said.

"You're right. She'll be a mess. This is a total violation of her personal space. What a fucking creep. We have to find him. No woman is safe with a guy like this around," Taylor said.

Mike made the call and quickly explained to Danny what happened then he hung up the phone.

"Everyone needs to step up their protection over the women," Mike whispered as he looked around, being sure not to touch anything.

"No problems there. We've got Marlena's friends covered. If this guy got this close into town, he could get his hands on Marlena's friends or people she's close to," Taylor said then pulled out his personal phone and texted someone.

"Texting your brothers about Mercedes?" Mike asked as they heard the cars pulling up outside.

"You betcha, and she isn't going to take it well, believe me."

Mike chuckled.

"You guys should take it as an opportunity to make a move. You know you're interested in her," Mike said.

"Yeah, well, it's going to take some time. There are things to work out, first."

"What's going on?" the sheriff asked as he walked through the open front door.

"Looks like a break-in. The asshole is in town. He left a note," Mike said.

"Shit. Did you call your brothers?" the sheriff asked Mike.

"Danny is with Marlena at the diner."

"You have a forensics team on hand?" Detective Morgan asked as he entered the cottage.

"We get help from the state police five miles out of town."

"Call it in. We need all the concrete evidence we can get against this guy to prove he's a criminal and intent on doing harm to Marlena. I need fingerprints, hair follicles, something concrete."

"How about this?" The sheriff asked as he pointed to the floor on the other side of the bed. Mike walked around as well as Detective Morgan.

Mike clenched his teeth and felt about ready to explode.

A pair of Marlena's panties were in a ball on the floor and there looked to be something wet on them.

"I hope the stupid son of a bitch was dumb enough to jerk off in those. Sorry, Mike," the detective said, and Mike nodded his head and tried to control his fuming temper. This guy was sick, blatant, and unafraid of the law. He felt the hand on his shoulder.

"Let's wait outside. The forensics team will be here soon, we all need to work on a plan to go hunting," Taylor said, and Mike agreed. This wasn't a normal case. Not just because it was his girlfriend involved but because this guy Peter appeared to believe he was above the law and could get away with doing anything he wanted to try and get to Marlena. He felt sick to his stomach. The guy fucking went through her panties, maybe jerked off in them, and was on her bed. It was becoming pretty clear that Peter needed to be stopped before someone else got hurt. They couldn't leave Marlena alone. They had to protect her no matter what. They had to.

* * * *

What do you mean I can't go back to the cottage? Why the hell not?" Marlena asked as she got into the SUV with Danny and Jack. She was sitting in the middle between them.

They were being very quiet and yet they were touching her every chance they had and even kissing her or looking at her with soft expressions. But what also caught her attention was the way Jack kept looking in his rearview mirror and side mirrors as if seeing if someone was following them.

"What in God's name is going on? Just tell me already," she said.

"Nothing is going on. Let's head to our place. You can shower and change and we'll make some dinner," Danny told her.

"I need more clothes. I've been wearing the same things over and over again the last two weeks." She raised her voice and both men were quiet. Both men had firm expressions and seemed to be half paying attention to her. She saw Jack look in the rearview mirror again and this time Danny looked at the side mirror.

She looked over her shoulder trying to see what they could be looking at.

"Why do you keep doing that? Are you looking for someone?" she asked just as they saw multiple state police vehicles pass by them in the opposite direction.

Looking back, it appeared as if they were headed into the center of town.

"What was that all about?" she asked and Danny looked at Jack. Jack gripped the steering wheel tighter.

"Jack?" She pushed, and touched his forearm. He was tense, hard, angry. She gulped and pulled back. This wasn't his normal demeanor.

Then it hit her. The police cars, the state police, the two of them acting funny and not letting her go to her own cottage, and all the chaos as she exited the diner tonight. Peter was in the area and they knew it.

She covered her mouth and felt the tears emerge just as Jack made the turn down the long dirt road that led to their property. The sheriff's patrol car was there along with Detective Morgan's.

Jack pulled the truck to a stop and Danny took her hand.

"We won't let him get to you, Marlena. We will protect you."

"Tell me what happened. Did someone see Peter nearby? Did he do something?"

"Help her out of the vehicle. We'll discuss everything that's going on inside with Mike."

Jack looked so pissed off. It made her feel unsteady as Danny helped her from the SUV.

Everyone looked at her and Detective Morgan approached.

"Mike, the sheriff, and Taylor and I went over the entire house. Everything looks secure. She'll be safe here when she's not at work."

"She's not going back to the diner. Not until this nutjob is caught," Jack stated firmly.

"What? Wait a minute. Someone tell me what's happening here."

"You didn't explain things to her?" Detective Morgan asked.

Jack and Danny looked at Mike as he approached.

"I asked them not to."

"Mike, what happened?"

Mike looked her over but kept his distance. At first she felt insulted, upset that he would deny any affection of relationship's status in front of the detective and the others, but then she realized by the expressions around her that they were all affected by whatever happened and Mike was in police mode.

"We have reason to believe that Peter is in the vicinity," Mike told her.

She covered her mouth and took a step back. Jack was there to hold her as she leaned against him.

"How do you know?"

Mike looked away. It appeared as if he bit the inside of his cheek and had to gain some composure.

"He broke into your cottage."

She was shocked as she shook her head and felt the tears fill her eyes.

"How do you know?"

"He left a note. He tore apart your clothes and trashed the place, and he left other evidence that the state police forensics team collected and is bringing to the lab to analyze."

"Evidence? Like what?" she asked.

Mike shook his head.

"It's not really necessary to get into," the sheriff said, sounding just as ticked off as Mike and looking like he knew what was left and didn't want to say.

"It's important that you understand we need to step up security around you. We'll find him. We're organizing a team to help search both by vehicle and on ATVs," Taylor added.

She knew whatever was left it really affected the men so she dropped it for now.

"Let's get you inside," Jack said and she looked at Mike as Danny joined her on the other side like they were her personal body protectors. What did they think, Peter would try to shoot and kill them like some sniper?

As she thought the thought she looked around them and toward the abundance of woods surrounding their home. She hurried to the door with Jack and Danny. Her concern was for them. She wouldn't let anything happen to them.

They went into the house and she didn't feel so good. Her emotions, her anxiety about their behavior was getting the better of her.

She felt the hands on her shoulders. *Danny.*

"Why don't you go shower and change into something more comfortable? We'll start dinner. It's getting late."

She looked toward the windows of the house and could see the sunlight slowly disappearing. The cars and trucks were leaving but Mike was still out there. Alone.

Danny guided her upstairs.

"I'm fine. I can do it myself," she told him. She was upset. They were obviously keeping things from her and she didn't like it at all. They asked her to be honest with them and she was. She didn't hold back, especially not these last few weeks.

She started to unbutton her blouse when Danny turned her around and pulled her into a hug against his chest. She felt his heart racing. She heard him breathing heavily, inhaling her shampoo as he used his hands to squeeze against her ass and pull her to him.

"I love you so much, Marlena."

She listened to him breathing. The way he paused and squeezed her as he said those words.

"I love you, too."

"This guy is bad news. He wants to hurt you. He left things at your cottage. He did things to your... God, I hate this," he said and pulled back.

He held her gaze.

"What things? What did he leave? What do you mean? Why won't any of you tell me?"

He stared down into her eyes.

"He lay on your bed. He touched your panties. He...Fuck." He pulled her close and kissed her deeply. It was as if he was trying to get the images out of her head. She held him tight and she thought about what he didn't say. What he couldn't say. Peter was on her bed. He did things. He touched her panties. What had he done to them?

He released her lips slowly and then controlled his breathing.

"Let's get the shower ready. I'll help you. I need to be inside of you, baby. I need to be that close."

He undressed her and she undressed him then they got into the shower together.

Danny didn't hesitate. He washed her up, making her skin soft and covered in lathered soap. He turned her around to help rinse her body and then he turned her back to face him.

"I need you." He cupped her breasts then leaned forward and kissed her lips. She reached between them and stroked his cock, She ran her sudsy fingers back and forth over the ridge and then to his testicles and massaged them. He kissed her deeply and moaned into her mouth.

In a flash his fingers were stroking her cunt, bringing her juices out to lubricate her channel.

The water flowed between them, washing away the remainder of suds and cascading them in warmth. His kisses grew deeper, more demanding, and then he lifted her up and pressed her against the tiled wall.

She maneuvered his cock toward her pussy and sank down on the thick, hard muscle. Tilting her head back, she moaned and he began to thrust and rock his cock deeper and faster into her pussy.

"I love how you feel inside of me. Everything is perfect," she told him, and he growled out almost in anger.

His face wedged against the crook of her neck and his mouth suckled hard against her skin. He gripped her hips and stroked harder, faster into her.

"You're mine. All mine. No one can ever have this body, have your orgasms, your pleasure but my brothers and me." His strokes were so hard, so deep she cried out in ecstasy.

"Yes. Yes, Danny, all yours and Mike's and Jack's. Only you," she told him as a feeling of possessiveness and need shot through her system. She ran her fingers through his hair, she counterthrust against him, and then she felt her entire body tighten as she screamed her release and Danny growled out his against her neck. The water splashed between their bodies as skin collided against skin in those last few strokes. Then they held one another close and she relished in the way she felt with him inside of her and the connection that could never be severed.

"I love you, forever," she whispered and she hugged him tight until the water cooled and they were forced to step back out into reality.

* * * *

"I can't get the fucking image out of my mind. I can't. I tried, but it's no use. I see that fucking asshole's face from the picture in my head. Then I see her bedroom, the way he slept on her bed as if he were waiting for her. The worst, the fucking panties, a bunch of them scattered, ripped on the floor and on the bed, then the one pair on the rug. The ones he jerked off in thinking about our woman. Our Marlena." Mike raised his voice and slammed his hand down onto the island in the kitchen.

"Damn it, I fucking can't even imagine. The sheriff is pissed off, Taylor looks ready to kill someone, and poor Marlena doesn't know any of this. We need to tell her. She needs to understand that she has to stay with us and be surrounded by people who can protect her until this dick is found," Jack told his brother.

"I know. Believe me, I fucking know but I can't talk to her right now and explain. I have to be part of the search crew. I need you and Danny to stay with her."

"Mike, she needs you, too. If you walk out of here tonight to go search for this guy without first talking to her and letting her know what happened and how you feel then she's going to distance herself from you."

"What do you mean? Why? She knows I'm a cop, that I need to be part of this."

"She doesn't know anything because you haven't told her shit. Danny took her upstairs to shower and change. You need to clear the air and let her know what you're doing and how much you love her."

"What's going on?" Danny asked, joining them at the kitchen counter. It was dark out. Dinner was cooking in the pan. Mike just wanted to explore the feelings him and his brothers had for Marlena and not be facing a situation like this. The guy was taunting the police, basically saying that he didn't think they could catch him. It was like he thought he had the upper hand. That was what really pissed Mike off. Who the hell was this guy and how did he get away with all the things he did and not get caught? He was barely questioned by police. He looked at Danny.

"Where is Marlena?" Mike asked.

"She had a headache. She's laying down a bit. I told her we would wake her to eat in a little while. So maybe you'd like to explain in better detail about today, and what the plan is so we can find this asshole and take him out," Danny said to Mike.

Mike took a deep breath and released it.

"Now is a better time as any to explain things to us. The three of us need to be on the same page about this guy. What's the plan of action? Is anyone looking for him right now?" Danny asked.

"There's a team out right now. They're casing the wooded areas, and a little far north into the mountains in case he's hiding out there. So far no word on anything yet," Mike told them, and he explained about Marlena's cottage, about Peter's note, combined with what they already knew from Detective Morgan.

"So this other team, the one you want to be part of, is going out in the morning?" Danny asked.

"About four a.m. The sheriff got a hold of his friends in the K-9 unit. They feel they can get a great scent of Peter from the bedsheets and other items he touched," Mike told them and ran his fingers through his hair.

"Great. When do they start?" Jack asked.

"They should have by now. Maybe we'll get lucky and it will lead us right to the fucker," Mike said, and Danny and Jack agreed then talked a little more about tomorrow and how they would protect their woman from this monster.

* * * *

Marlena threw on a pair of shorts and a tank top. She lay down on the bed after drying her hair. She needed time to think, and to process what was happening here.

As she closed her eyes and thought about her men. She felt how much she adored them and just wanted to get lost in their arms, with the three of them making love to her together and making her feel complete and finally loved.

The past wasn't quite behind her. Sure she made mistakes. Hell, she was paying for the biggest mistake right now. Falling for Peter, a man who manipulated her mind, controlled her every move, and eventually tried to kill her. Now he was back. Searching, possibly in this town. A town she had grown to love, to appreciate, and wanted to remain in. Her heart felt heavy. Especially thinking that she was placing so many other people in danger because of her. It wasn't right.

But she loved it in Chance. She loved Mike, Danny, and Jack so much. They showed her what love really was and she wanted to learn more and explore more with them. She never thought about having children with Peter. It was like she knew deep down that he didn't love her like that. He obsessed over her like a possession. But with Mike, Danny, and Jack, she wanted to have children. She wanted to share that bond, God's creation with all their qualities combined. She didn't care how it worked. She'd love them and honor them and be the best wife they could ever ask for. She could have it all.

She felt the gentle breeze caress through the open window. It was a warm summer night, and normally she would have sat on her back porch at her cottage and enjoyed the quietness. But tonight she sensed something different, something that had her opening her eyes and feeling scared to be alone. It was on the tip of the breeze that caressed her body as it snuck through the opening in the window. It put her on edge. It made her feel a fight in her she hadn't felt before. Was she being protective of her new lovers, the men she adored with all her heart? How could she protect them?

She sat up, listened carefully, barely hearing the sounds of anything but the breeze as it caused the curtain to flap against the window sill.

It was quiet. Too quiet, and she suddenly longed for the touch from her men. The protective shell they seemed to wrap her in whenever they were near.

She placed her feet on the floor and felt her heart begin to race. She wanted her men. She needed them. They would protect her, make her feel safe and loved, and she couldn't stand to be away.

As she began to stand, she heard the creak on the floor and went to turn, shocked at the sudden sound, but it was too late. The hand went over her mouth, the hard, fierce fingers dug deep, gripped her hair, and pulled her backward. She struggled but a moment as her eyes locked onto Peter's. He looked wild, sadistic as she kicked her legs and scratched at his face.

He straddled her on the bed.

"I'll kill them. I have the house rigged with explosives. I'll burn them to death while we watch from afar. Do you understand me?"

She felt the tears roll down her cheeks. He was so heavy and hard against her chest as he covered her body. She nodded.

"You cooperate, and they'll live. Unless you want them to die along with you?" he asked, teeth clenched, his spittle hitting her lips. She was disgusted, scared, sick with fear. She nodded. She would do anything to protect Mike, Jack, and Danny. She had to do this. It wasn't right for them to get hurt or die because of her.

"Get up, and do as I say."

He eased off of her, but his hold was firm. He immediately wrapped a bandana around her mouth and tied it tight so she couldn't scream for help or make the men aware of his presence. Obviously they hadn't set the alarms yet. They did that at night before they went to bed. Her men were right down stairs and she couldn't call to them. She wouldn't let Peter hurt them. She knew what he was capable of. She needed to do something, but she couldn't allow him to hurt them. She obeyed his command, especially as he pulled the knife from his hip and held it to her throat.

"Not a sound," he whispered.

She never saw it coming. She didn't know what he did, but she felt the pinch to her neck and she reached up to cover the spot. She looked at him, eyes wide, and saw the expression of pleasure, or accomplishment, as her vision blurred and her body went limp. Darkness overtook her. He won. She was as good as dead.

* * * *

"What did you just say?" Mike said into his cell phone as him and his brothers prepared dinner. Danny was heading upstairs to wake Marlena.

He placed the phone on speaker.

"The dogs caught a scent. We've been traveling through the woods. He's somewhere on your property. We've pulled them back and we're on the outskirts," Taylor told him.

"Danny, get Marlena. We'll bring her to the basement and protect her from there," he called to his brother.

"Hold them back, Taylor. We don't want to spook him. If he's going to try and break in to get her we need to be ready," Mike said and nodded toward Jack. Jack went to the cabinet on the wall that looked like a bookcase. He pressed on the button to the side and the bookshelf began to move. Jack started pulling guns from the shelves.

"Mike! Mike! She's gone. There's a needle on the bed. I think he got her. Oh God! I think Peter has her," Danny yelled.

"What?" Jack yelled out and he ran up the stairs behind Mike.

"What is it? What's wrong?" Taylor asked, still on speakerphone.

Mike looked at the messed up covers, the needle on the bed and the one shoe on the rug.

"Fuck! He has her, Taylor. Peter took Marlena, right out from under our noses."

"Fuck!" Danny kicked the dresser, making it rock and almost tip over.

"Get your gear and get out here. The dogs are picking up on the scent. They'll find her. Bring out something she was wearing," Taylor said and Jack grabbed her light sweater. He brought it to his nose, closed his eyes, and smelled her scent.

"We have to find her fast, Mike. He'll kill her."

"We will. I won't let him take her from us. I won't," Mike said.

Danny picked up the shotgun he placed on the dresser and held it against him. "We're not going to let him kill our woman. Let's move."

* * * *

Marlena felt her head pounding. She moaned and realized instantly that she was tied to something. Her eyes and nostrils burned. Was that gasoline she smelled?

She blinked her eyes open and saw Peter watching her. He'd doused the place in gasoline. She was going to burn to death.

She cried out and tried to pull her hands and legs from the confinement of the rope.

"Help me! Help!" she screamed and struggled.

He struck her with a backhand.

She screamed at him.

"I hate you! You sick son of a bitch. They'll get you and when they do you'll die a miserable painful death."

He struck her again and again. Her vision blurred and he pulled back and spat at her.

"You're nothing. They're nothing. I'm going to watch you burn and then I'm going to watch the three men you've been screwing watch you die."

"Fuck you!"

"You deserve to die. Screwing three men. I heard you with him in the fucking shower. You bitch."

"That's right. I was making love to him, just like I made love to his brothers."

He straddled her waist and tore her T-shirt apart.

"You're going to pay for that. You can't fight me. You're weak and this time you're going to die. I can take anything, everything away from you, Marlena. I've told you that over and over again back home. You belong to me. I molded you into the woman I wanted you to be."

"You didn't mold shit. If I was the woman you wanted me to be, then why did you cheat on me?"

He smacked her again and she cried out in pain.

"I have needs, Marlena. I wanted you pure and perfect. But I see now, that you're fucking three men like some whore, that I misread you. You weren't worth my time. Then you tried to run from me. Like you could do that. Like you had control. Never. I'm the one that can give you life or death. I will always have control over you. Always."

"You're sick, and you're evil. I'm my own person. You knew that. That's why you cheated on me and tried to kill me. But you lost everything. You lost the slut you were screwing and you lost your control of me," she said to him, feeling her lip drip blood and her cheek ache something terrible. Her eye was swelling closed and she was shocked when he gripped her by the throat and started choking her.

She kicked and struggled to get free. He leaned forward, hands on her throat still, and kissed her. He plunged his tongue in deep and she was desperate for breath, to live. She didn't know what to do when she bit into his tongue.

He struck her, instantly releasing his hold on her neck. The strikes went everywhere as he battered and beat her until she couldn't move.

She lost. He won. Her vision blurred, the tears flowed, the weakness was overpowering, and she lost her ability to see.

She heard a noise. She saw the flash of a lighter and Peter smiling.

"Who won now, Marlena? Who always wins?"

He tossed the lighter to the corner and instantly fire began to flow up the wall. It would be minutes before it reached her on the bed. She was going to die.

She looked at him, knowing that he felt triumphant and as if he truly won.

"You didn't win anything. I don't love you. I never did, but I love them. My three men, and that's what you can always remember about me. My last words before I die. I love Jack, Mike, and Danny forever!" she yelled, voice cracking, everything aching, and the fight leaving her body, forcing her eyes to close.

* * * *

"Run, goddamn it. I see smoke!" Danny yelled as the multiple police cars, ATVs, and regular trucks made it to the log cabin in the woods twenty minutes from their house. The dogs almost lost the scent, but as they searched for close locations that Peter could have taken her to, another group with dogs picked up on a scent down the dirt road that led to the cabin. They found her. But the cabin was already showing signs of fire.

They all ran as fast as they could. Mike, Danny, and Jack barreled through the door along with their friends and fellow community members.

Danny saw Marlena. The fire nearly at the bed she was tied to. She was beaten and battered. Unconscious from either the smoke of the damage done to her body. Him and Jack ran to her to cut the ropes. But Mike roared in anger and headed to the side. Danny and Jack never even saw Peter. Their focus was solely on getting to Marlena and saving her. She didn't move at all. He heard yelling, a struggle then glanced to the right. Peter rushed at Mike and the two fought. Jack was untying Marlena and Danny felt filled with fear for his brother and for their woman. They could hear the scuffle then the sound of a gun going off had Danny and Jack pressing over Marlena's body in a protective shield. Danny saw the gun on the floor and then Peter reach for it.

"She'll die and all of you will too."

"Freeze! Give it up. It's over." The sheriff yelled toward Pete, gun drawn. Taylor and the others had their guns drawn too and then Mike did some serious combat moves, manipulated the gun from Peter's hands, and reached for it. Danny watched Mike fall backward then shoot at Peter as Peter lunged for Mike's throat. The gun went off. Peter lay on the floor, a bullet to his head.

"We have to move. The fire is moving too quickly. The fire department is on its way. They won't make it in time," the sheriff yelled and helped them along with Taylor to cut the ropes.

"Oh God, look at her. She's all bruised and cut. What the fuck did he do to her?" Jack asked as Danny slowly went to lift her.

He got her into his arms. She was limp, barely breathing as Jack checked her pulse. As he stepped from the house with his brothers, a sea of law enforcement and friends were there. All carrying weapons. All ready to protect one of their own.

"An ambulance is on its way," Taylor told him, his expression like everyone else's. Shock, disgust, perhaps feelings of failure like Danny was feeling.

The sound of sirens blaring filled the air. The lights from the ambulance could be seen coming up the dirt road quickly. As he stopped short, and the paramedics got out, even they were members of Chance.

"Please. You have to save her. Help her," Danny said to them.

"Jesus. What the hell happened to her?" the paramedic asked as they helped her onto the gurney and began to look over her injuries to see what were more serious.

"We have to get her to the ER. Her pulse is really weak. She could have internal bleeding from the way her ribs and neck are bruising and swelling. We need to move," the paramedic said, and they strapped her in and began to get her into the ambulance.

"Go with her, Danny. We'll follow," Mike said and Danny nodded and then jumped into the back of the ambulance.

The doors closed and he saw his brothers' eyes and their friends' expressions. They all might have been too late. All he kept thinking was that he never should have left her upstairs alone. If he hadn't, maybe he could have fought off Peter and saved Marlena. She was his responsibility. She was their woman and they claimed her, took guardianship over her, yet they failed her and it could cost her her life.

He held her hand and covered his mouth with his hand as tears filled his eyes.

He'd finally found the perfect woman to love, to complete the bond between him and his brothers, and he ruined it. They all did. They failed terribly.

* * * *

"It's not your fault. None of us expected that he was already in the house hiding. We looked everywhere. It was out of your control, so stop beating yourselves up over it. She's going to pull through," Sheriff Max Gordon told Mike, Danny, and Jack. But they didn't want to hear it. For several days, Marlena lay unconscious. The doctors worked on running tests and finding out what drug Peter had given her. Whatever it was, she suffered an adverse effect from it and it sent her into a coma. The doctors didn't think that was a bad thing, considering the injuries to her ribs, and the severity of the damage to her esophagus. She had a breathing tube, was sedated to help her heal, and an I.V. of fluids and nutrients was constantly going.

Mike ran his fingers through his hair as he stared at Marlena. She was white as a ghost. She looked frail and weak. It brought tears to his eyes every day he came here and sat with her. His brothers weren't saying much. When they talked, they fought. They argued about leaving her alone, about failing as her guardians and about not having what it took to care for her and love her and protect her the way she deserved. Everything was falling apart.

"Boys." They all looked up when they heard their mom's voice. The sheriff left the room and their dads stood outside in the waiting area.

She had been a total mess when she first saw Marlena lying in the hospital bed with all the tubes and monitors going. Even Marlena's friends, Alicia, Mercedes, and Adele cried. They would be by again shortly. They came by on their lunch breaks every day and at dinnertime after they left work. Marlena had so many visitors. So many people loved her and wanted her to heal and get better. Her room was covered with balloons and flowers, and she couldn't open her eyes to see any of it.

Their mom walked past Danny and went to the side of the bed. She reached out and caressed Marlena's hand then leaned down and kissed her cheek.

"Okay, little lady, you've got everyone in a state of panic and fear right now. I need you to wake up, and to fight for what you want," she told her and smiled. She reached out and caressed her cheek.

She looked at Mike and his brothers.

"The three of you need to get over this cockamamie belief that you failed her. You did no such thing. You saved her before that man could kill her and you killed him, ensuring she would be safe forever. Now, you are the three most stubborn, toughest men I know aside from your fathers. I don't expect you to keep this nonsense up. Marlena loves you and you love her. She survived. She's going to get through this and you have everyone's support in it. I want you to get cleaned up, shave those whiskers so that when Marlena awakes, she'll smile at seeing her handsome men."

"Mom, she hasn't awoken for days. It's not that easy, anyway," Danny told her.

"It's our fault that she's there. She was under our protection, in our house when he broke in and took her. We hadn't a clue," Jack said.

"And you two had a clue when Mickey Joe was stealing money from the register at Spencer's for months? You had a clue when he was bringing in women and using your office as a private screw room while you two trusted him?" she said to them.

"Mom, that's not the same thing." Danny said.

"It's not? You're supposed to distrust every person and not leave them alone to take care of simple tasks and do their job without babysitting them? How have you succeeded in life?" she asked.

"We left her alone knowing he was in the vicinity," Danny said.

"You left her upstairs, in your own house while she rested while you cooked her dinner. The sheriff said they all checked the house. He was that resourceful, that sneaky and conniving that he got to her. It wasn't your fault. You were planning the next steps in trying to protect her. It was a window of opportunity to strike. You know this, too, Mike. You're a deputy, you were a SEAL. Did every mission go as planned? Did the people you were sent in to take out, to rescue or to pull in for whatever reason, always where they were supposed to be or where you were told? Did you need to improvise and adapt? This situation was no different. That man got into your house long before any of you even arrived. He found a good hiding spot and he waited while you went about taking care of Marlena and ensuring she rested before dinner. It's not your fault. The end result was that you saved her before she was killed, burned to death in some cabin by the man that tried taking everything away from all of you.

"She's your woman. You love her and she loves you. When she comes out of this she is going to be a mess. She's going to be scared, timid. She'll probably have nightmares and fear being alone. You three will need to protect her, console her, be patient with her, and build up her confidence again so she can live a normal life. A happy life with the three of you. Don't you love her and want her forever?" their mom asked.

"Of course we do," Jack said.

"Then don't waste any more time feeling guilty or thinking about the what-ifs. Concern yourselves with loving her. With being the men she more than deserves after the heartache, the pain, and fear she's experienced in life thus far. Be the men that I and your fathers know you can be for her, and love her, with all your heart and soul. It will work out just fine. Believe me, she trusts you. She won't blame you for anything. In fact, I wouldn't be surprised if she cooperated in order to save the three of you from harm. Snap out of it. Your fathers and I raised good, honest, compassionate, strong men. She'll need you, and nothing else will matter."

Epilogue

Marlena sat on Danny's lap as they swung on the porch swing. It was a beautiful fall day and she finally felt stronger then she had in weeks.

Danny caressed her thigh and kissed her shoulder.

"I love it out here. You guys have a beautiful view," she said.

"You say that every time we sit out here. I think you like this porch swing better than the big sofa in the living room," he teased and she turned to look at him.

"I love being here with you, Mike, and Danny. You've helped me so much. I think I want to try to go back to the diner."

He scrunched his eyebrows together.

"I don't know, Marlena. You're still working with the therapist and trying to deal with the nightmares."

"I'm doing better. I've only had two episodes this week," she said as she stood up and tuned to face him.

"It's only Wednesday," Jack said from the doorway.

She turned around, feeling frustrated. They were all so protective of her. She loved them for it. She needed to have them sleep with her and cuddle with her. She hadn't gone anywhere, not even to town, without one of them with her. But she knew she needed to get control of her life again. She needed to fight for her independence and not fear Peter, who was dead and could never hurt her again. It wasn't easy though.

She heard the door open and she knew it was probably Mike. She inhaled as the soft breeze caressed against her hair. She smelled his cologne and knew it was Mike. It was strange, but she could sense when they were near, she could pick out their colognes, their scents from everyone else's. God, she sounded obsessed with them.

She felt the arm go around her waist and Mike's lips kissed her neck.

"What's going on?" he asked.

She turned in his arms and hugged him. He caressed his palm along her ass, squeezing her tighter to him. She smiled.

"I missed you."

He chuckled low, his warm breath colliding against her neck.

"I missed you more," he said. It was a regular routine. Something they all shared with one another.

She pulled back.

"I was just talking with Danny. I think it's time I try to go back to work at the diner. Your mom said I could whenever I feel I'm ready. Maybe a day or two to start out. What do you think?" she asked.

He licked his lower lip and looked at Danny and Jack, who now stood on either side of Mike and held her gaze.

"I think if you feel that you're ready, that it's a great idea."

She smiled and looked at Danny.

He crossed his arms in front of his chest. He hardly went to work because he was worried about leaving her. They never left her alone for months now. It wasn't fair to him or to Jack and Mike.

She reached out and touched his arm.

"Danny, I love you, but it isn't fair that I keep you from your job and the edition you and Jack have been wanting to do."

"We've talked about this, baby. We're not taking that on. Not until you're a hundred percent better," Jack said.

"I'm almost there. You two can't hold out on your dreams because of me. There has to be a way to work this out."

They were all silent and then the thought hit her.

"You know that I was an accountant back in Connecticut and I have my license?" she asked.

Jack squinted his eyes at her but Mike smiled as if he knew where she was going with this.

"And?" Danny asked.

"Well, with business expanding you may need a little help with your accounting, and perhaps maintaining the books for Spencer's. Maybe you'd consider offering me a job?" she asked and winked.

"That's an awesome idea. I love it," Danny said and he pulled her into a hug and then kissed her.

"Wait one minute," Jack said and Danny released her. She was afraid that he was going to say he didn't want to hire her or that he didn't think she was capable. She felt the tears reach her eyes and she damned herself for being affected so easily. If she were going to get them to give her a little freedom to prove she was stronger, tearing up all the time wouldn't help.

Jack pulled her by her belt hoop closer to him.

He ran his hand along her hip then up to her breast, cupping it.

"I think we need to do a little investigating into your credentials and abilities to make sure you're able to complete tasks in a timely manner."

He pinched her nipple and she licked her lower lip and held his gaze.

Danny reached over and began to unzip her pants and pressed them down, using his fingers to locate her pussy.

"I can do a background check," Mike said, maneuvering in behind her and thrusting his hips against her ass. She felt his cock and she smiled.

"I can assure the three of you that I'm perfect for any position you need me in. In fact, my capabilities will impress you," she said and gasped as Danny maneuvered his fingers up into her cunt, while Mike spread her thighs with his thigh, making her step into a wider stance.

"What type of capabilities are we talking about, Miss. Courts?" Jack asked and he lifted her top, unclipped her bra, and cupped both sensitive, full breasts.

"I take orders well, sir. Plus I like to think out of the box." She reached toward Jack's pants and unzipped them, then pushed them down and cupped his balls.

"I think we need a demonstration," Danny told her.

She immediately lowered to her knees, bent forward, and pulled Jack's cock between her lips. She stroked it with her tongue, twirled her tongue around it then pinched his balls.

Jack gripped her hair and began to thrust into her mouth. Behind her, Mike stroked her cunt and then she felt his fingers press against her clit. She came hard, nearly losing focus on Jack's cock.

But then she reached to the side and worked Danny's cock over his jeans. He unzipped them and whipped out the thick hard muscle and she slowly released Jack's cock and then took Danny's into her mouth.

She suckled back and forth between them as both men allowed her to pleasure them one after the other.

"Oh sweet Jesus, baby. You're hired," Jack said, and Danny and Mike chuckled.

Marlena smiled to herself. She loved them so much. She would give them the world if she had that capability. But for now, she would love them with all her heart and treasure every waking moment they shared.

She finally learned to trust again, and with that trust she gave her heart and soul to Jack, Danny, and Mike. Her lovers, her best friends, her destiny in a town called Chance.

THE END

WWW.DIXIELYNNDWYER.COM

ABOUT THE AUTHOR

People seem to be more interested in my name than where I get my ideas for my stories from. So I might as well share the story behind my name with all my readers.

My momma was born and raised in New Orleans. At the age of twenty, she met and fell in love with an Irishman named Patrick Riley Dwyer. Needless to say, the family was a bit taken aback by this as they hoped she would marry a family friend. It was a modern day arranged marriage kind of thing and my momma downright refused.

Being that my momma's families were descendents of the original English speaking Southerners, they wanted the family blood line to stay pure. They were wealthy and my father's family was poor.

Despite attempts by my grandpapa to make Patrick leave and destroy the love between them, my parents married. They recently celebrated their sixtieth wedding anniversary.

I am one of six children born to Patrick and Lynn Dwyer. I am a combination of both Irish and a true Southern belle. With a name like Dixie Lynn Dwyer it's no wonder why people are curious about my name.

Just as my parents had a love story of their own, I grew up intrigued by the lifestyles of others. My imagination as well as my need to stray from the straight and narrow made me into the woman I am today.

For all titles by Dixie Lynn Dwyer, please visit
www.bookstrand.com/dixie-lynn-dwyer

Siren Publishing, Inc.
www.SirenPublishing.com

Lightning Source UK Ltd.
Milton Keynes UK
UKOW06f1933070915

258236UK00020B/508/P